The Girl with the Golden Parasol

The Girl with the Golden Parasol

UDAY PRAKASH

TRANSLATED BY JASON GRUNEBAUM

YALE UNIVERSITY PRESS ■ NEW HAVEN & LONDON

A MARGELLOS
WORLD REPUBLIC OF LETTERS BOOK

The Margellos World Republic of Letters is dedicated to making literary works from around the globe available in English through translation. It brings to the English-speaking world the work of leading poets, novelists, essayists, philosophers, and playwrights from Europe, Latin America, Africa, Asia, and the Middle East to stimulate international discourse and creative exchange.

Yale University Press books may be purchased in quantity for educational, business, or promotional use. For information, please e-mail sales.press@yale.edu (U.S. office) or sales@yaleup.co.uk (U.K. office).

Printed in the United States of America.

Library of Congress Cataloging-in-Publication Data
Udaya Prakasa, 1951–
[Pīlī chatrī vālī laṛakī. English]
The girl with the golden parasol / Uday Prakash ; translated by Jason Grunebaum.
    pages cm. — (The Margellos world republic of letters)
ISBN 978-0-300-19054-0 (pbk. with flaps : alk. paper)
I. Grunebaum, Jason, translator. II. Title.
PK2098.41.D33P5513 2013
891.4'3371—dc23   2012042140

A catalogue record for this book is available from the British Library.

This paper meets the requirements of ANSI/NISO Z39.48–1992 (Permanence of Paper).

10 9 8 7 6 5 4 3 2 1

In memory of the secular solitude of the late Nirmal Verma: the quiet, upright "expatriate"

and

To my friend and Hindi publisher Arun Maheshwari, who provided me the ways and means to complete the book

CONTENTS

INTRODUCTION

Rahul, a non-Brahmin college boy, falls in love with Anjali, a Brahmin girl. This shouldn't be a problem in today's modern India of shopping malls, cell phones, and high tech, right? Surely the new forces of progress have begun to level the ancient hierarchies of caste.

The news of these new forces—vast changes unleashed by the economic reforms of the 1990s—has steadily reached our shores. Liberalization has brought a steep rise in capital influx and mass consumerism to an Indian society that is, in many ways, now utterly transformed. Call centers, cheap cars, job growth from outsourcing, and a flourishing IT sector have shaped a new image of India in the eyes of the West, while tales of Indians on the move and romantic rags-to-riches stories still compete with familiar pieces about the "old" India: poverty, corruption, riots. Those who can keep up with the aggressive market prosper, while others who don't get with the program may be marked for extinction, according to Uday Prakash in his short story "The Walls of Delhi": "The poor, the sick, the street corner prophets, the lowly, the unexceptional—all gone! They've vanished from this new Delhi of wealth and wizardry, never to return, not here, not anywhere."

The visible changes in India are apparent to everyone, and lend themselves to vivid contemporary accounts across fiction, cinema, and journalism. *The Girl with the Golden Parasol* joins this conversation as a dark statement warning of the fragile human riches in danger of being eradicated by hungry capitalism. In the meantime, those on the move and those left behind are engaged in a struggle for India's future. Uday Prakash asks which of the two will be ascendant in the next generation: "The one with a Pepsi in hand, half-naked model on his arm, Visa card in the pocket; or him, the one with red eyes, whose parents have been plundered for fifty years by successive regimes, who has a weapon in hand and is killed every day in [police and paramilitary] 'encounters'?"

Change, as always, comes with stasis, and the visible coexists with the hidden, the concealed. *The Girl with the Golden Parasol* is an invective against the destructive power of predatory markets, but what gives the book its "weight and wings," to borrow a phrase from Susan Sontag, is its foregrounding of caste. Caste is the thing that hasn't changed, but is much more difficult for Western observers of India to make out. Is it like class? Race? Both? Neither?

The deep examination of caste in *The Girl with the Golden Parasol* is news from a world not to be found in popular accounts of exotic India flush with overripe mangos. It's true that in big cities and particularly among the cosmopolitan beneficiaries of liberalization and globalization, caste can matter a great deal less, or not at all. But the uncomfortable reality is that for a great majority of Indians, despite modernization and widespread access to consumer goods, it still matters quite a bit.

One of the accomplishments of *The Girl with the Golden Parasol* is the fictional space created by Prakash that allows those getting ahead and those left behind to face off against one another, but with a significant twist: the battle lines of conflict aren't drawn between the usual "us" versus "them": rich and poor, landowners and the landless, modern and traditional, developers and slum dwellers. It's all of these groups versus all of these groups simultaneously, but with the dynamics between expected foes infinitely complicated by the fact of caste.

It's difficult to find an analogy that comes close to capturing the feelings of vulnerability among the students depicted in *The Girl with the Golden Parasol*, but imagine a group of educated, Western, cosmopolitan kids from various socioeconomic backgrounds and of different races trapped in a brutal summer camp run by corrupt zealots. This might be a start. What Prakash dramatizes so well throughout the novel is how caste can intrude into every facet of Indian society, from love and sex to language and literature—and does intrude in ways largely absent from today's tales of India.

The writing of *The Girl with the Golden Parasol* began with some arm-twisting. *Hans*, the premier Hindi literary magazine established in 1930 by Premchand, the father of modern Hindi and Urdu fiction, was revived in the mid-1980s by the writer and editor Rajendra Yadav. The magazine was publishing a fifteenth-anniversary issue in 1999. Yadav asked Prakash if he would contribute to the issue, but at the time Prakash, though by then already a well-known Hindi fiction writer and poet, was busy doing what paid the bills: filming a documentary. After much insisting, Yadav prevailed upon Prakash, and he began writing what he thought would be a humorous love story. But as he wrote with the deadline looming, "everything began oozing out," in Prakash's words: a failed youthful love affair with a Brahmin girl (Prakash is a non-Brahmin) and caste politics that "do not allow love or anything humane to happen." He couldn't settle on an ending, so it was decided that the story would continue in serialized form.

Reader response to the story, as it unfolded over four issues in *Hans*, was dramatic. An extraordinary number of low-caste readers sent postcards, text messages, and even called Prakash to express their enthusiasm. (It's a near-universal practice to publish cell phone numbers of Hindi writers with their bios.) *Hans* was bought in bulk and distributed among this group of readers, many of whom began referring to *The Girl with the Golden Parasol* as their Bible.

This reaction made it clear to Prakash, who had not yet finished the serialized novel, that "it could not remain a love story . . . it was becoming something else." In an interesting interplay between an author and his readers, and perhaps fortified by their reaction, Prakash forged ahead with his full-throated critique of how the forces of globalization in India, instead of providing people with means of empowerment and mobility, have rather served to further strengthen the centuries-old domination of those at the top of the caste ladder—what Prakash in the novel calls "Brahminism" as a shorthand.

At the same time, Prakash realized that he had unintentionally done something "blasphemous" when he received quite a different kind of response in various Hindi newspapers and magazines. Stern words were used against him in the media. He was called a "mad dog" and "insane" not only by critics and academics but also by police officers and high-ranking officials in the Indian civil service. (People from all walks of life in India take part in public conversations about literature.) Unhappy with Prakash's novel, they targeted him personally. More disturbingly, over two dozen of his freelance TV, film, and writing assignments were cancelled almost overnight. Prakash, by foregrounding caste in his book, had clearly touched a nerve.

Here, as in many of his stories, Uday Prakash shows how those who dare to dissent against a suffocating system are punished. But the gloom and pall that hangs over the world in *The Girl with the Golden Parasol* is hardly the full story. With his biting satire and ambitious narrative detours Prakash also demonstrates how humor and compassion can provide one means to fight back and escape. Rahul, the protagonist of *The Girl with the Golden Parasol*, reconsiders the field of organic chemistry as his career path:

> What would he do with this degree? He'd become a chemist in a brewery or in a food-processing plant owned by some multinational company. Or he'd get a teaching position at a college or university. When he thought about his future, Rahul saw the image of a certain type of man take shape: fat, whiny, gobbling pizza slices like a pig, gnawing on morsels of scrumptious fish marinated in yogurt and vinegar, drinking and partying with a teenage girl he was paying by the hour, enticing her with a little dance of his by shaking his pot belly and gyrating his pumpkin-sized saggy ass.
>
> This type of man—a bottomless pit of lust and greed, a decadent cheat, gluttonous, licentious, corrupt—that's who

this country and system were set up to serve. All the shiny stores and legions of police and battalions of soldiers all exist to feed pleasure and stimulation to that man. If I work as an organic chemist, Rahul thought, I'll spend my whole life churning out yummy, lip-smacking, good-for-you consumables for *him*. This life, which the compassionate creator of the universe, acting with great kindness, has given, once and only once, to most negligible me.

The humor, polemics, and meanderings in the book are like *The Book of Laughter and Forgetting* blended with *Tristram Shandy* —and told by one of the most naturally gifted storytellers writing in any language. Among Hindi writers, Prakash, with his postmodern sensibility, has broken from a strict model of social realism that dominated Hindi fiction for much of the twentieth century, though his prose is full of lapidary detail from rural and mythical India that can only come from the mind of a writer deeply rooted to the land and its people. Prakash continues a tradition of satire recalling Hindi writers like Manohar Shyam Joshi, while inventing a humor that is all his own. As Robert Hueckstedt has written about Prakash's work in the introduction to his translation of Prakash stories entitled *Short Shorts Long Shots*, "Despite the seriousness of his purpose and commitment, he has never written a story, no matter how short, that does not make the reader smile or laugh."

After the backlash following *The Girl with the Golden Parasol*, life began to improve for Prakash. He published a wildly successful novella entitled *Mohandas* about a Dalit—untouchable—who tries to reclaim his identity stolen by an upper-caste identity thief.

An English translation of *The Girl with the Golden Parasol* was published in India, and the Indian national literary body, the Sahitya Akademi, awarded Uday Prakash its highest honor in Hindi for *Mohandas*. *Kindle* magazine named him a top South Asian youth icon, and his work continues to be translated into Urdu, Malayalam, Panjabi, Marathi, German, and Japanese.

I have had the great pleasure of knowing Uday Prakash personally since 2005, and over a series of my visits to India and his to the United States, we have developed an extraordinary working relationship and friendship. I am extremely grateful for his unwavering support of my translations of his work, and I am thrilled that American readers finally have the chance to hear the voice of one of India's most important and original writers.

Note on the Translation

Translation is a series of challenges and strategies, leading to possible solutions and, ultimately, choices, both large and small.

One of the challenges in translating *The Girl with the Golden Parasol* was the question of how to balance the needs of readers not particularly familiar with India with those who come to the book with a deeper knowledge of India and South Asia. What should I do in cases, for example, when I decided that there was a compelling reason to keep a word in Hindi? Footnotes and glossaries are two possible solutions. My general rule of thumb with footnotes is that if there were none in the original, I won't use any in the translation. Furthermore, footnotes suggest academic writing rather than literature. Glossaries divide the readers into two groups: one that needs to use the glossary, and the other that doesn't. Since I believe translation is an act of enlarging the conversation of literature, dividing readers into those who know and those who don't isn't in the spirit of why I translate. The solution I prefer, and the one I have broadly chosen to use in *The Girl with the Golden Parasol*, is to incorporate the needed information into the writing itself—a gloss within the text, a kind of "stealth gloss." Ideally, this gives readers who need it enough information and context to make sense of an unfamiliar word, while those who don't won't find the text too intrusive or "prechewed."

A related question is which English to write the translation in. American English? Indian English? If I were translating from, say, French or German, it wouldn't be necessary to consider the 250 million English speakers, and potential readers, of the English translation in France or Germany—or consider that the English spoken by these 250 million people has its own history, and is different in meaningful ways from North American and UK English idioms. Translators from Hindi and other South Asian languages do need, however, to think about what kind of English is most suitable. In *The Girl with the Golden Parasol*, I have written with an American audience foremost in my mind without, hopefully, neglecting the needs and expectations of a South Asian audience: I have called upon Americanisms as needed, and have drawn upon phrases and cadences from Indian English when appropriate. What I hope to have achieved is a creative hybridization —necessary for any work of translation from any language—that rewrites Prakash's Hindi into an English that realizes the voice, originality, and vitality of his prose.

Acknowledgments

I would like to thank the following people for their help in making this book possible: Uday Prakash and Kumkum, Becka McKay, Bob Hueckstedt, Esther Allen, Michael Henry Heim, Jennifer Lyons, John Donatich, Ulrike Stark, Valerie Ritter, Karen Hudes, Kelly Austin, Clint Seely, Idra Novey, Amit Chaudhuri, and Amitava Kumar.

I would also like to acknowledge the generous support of the PEN Translation Fund, whose award allowed me to travel to India to meet Uday for the first time.

Jason Grunebaum

The Girl with the Golden Parasol

ONE

Here's the bare backside of Madhuri Dixit, the same one Salman Khan had aimed at and hit with the pebble from his slingshot. Her back stiffened at the sting, she bent at the waist, and then turned around. Her gaze held no pain but rather a flirtatious excitement, inviting him toward her. The eyes didn't belong to Madhuri Dixit, but to a startled doe—an intoxicated, mad, silly doe who lovingly served herself up to her hunter.

Rahul had taped the photo, the center spread in that month's *Stardust*, on the window in his room. The blazing sun meant that afternoons on the second floor in Room 252 were hard to take. Madhuri Dixit's wounded bare backside repelled the intense rays of afternoon sun from his hostel room. She turned her head and stared nonstop at Rahul with those silly, drunken eyes, as if it'd been Rahul himself who'd made her beautiful wounded derriere a target.

Apart from Rahul, no one knew that during a private moment of utter secrecy, he'd had Salman Khan quietly removed from Room 252 and had himself taken the movie star's place. Rahul shivered with excitement as he realized that the man who had wounded Madhuri Dixit's gorgeous voluptuous backside was none other than he himself. It was his own slingshot that launched the pebble with a crack that whizzed into Madhuri Dixit, who then let loose an "Oooooooh!"—just as the image in *Stardust* had been snapped.

Girls enjoy being roughed up. They aren't chipmunks or kitty cats or small furry animals that purr and roll around when you pet them sweetly. A girl is a different kind of creature: the rougher it gets, the sharper the slap, the more she likes it.

The truth? Girls love brute strength.

That's why Rahul began working out at the school gym, in order to beef up his biceps like Salman Khan's. A core like a cheetah and upper body like a leopard. Rahul wanted to mold himself into a sleek, savage, fleet-footed wild animal. And then? Dark Ray-Bans, a pair of Wranglers or Levis, a T-shirt, and Nike socks to go with a winning pair of Woodland shoes.

He wondered why he didn't feel the same way gazing at Lara Datta, Manpreet Brar, or Gul Panag as he did looking at Madhuri. After all, Madhuri was quite a bit older than Rahul. He'd just seen a film with Miss World, Aishwarya Rai. Sure, she shook her bare backside and pranced around just like Madhuri, tilting her head from side to side, all the while staring at Rahul with her light brown eyes. But fuck, it was useless. Aishwarya didn't even come close. The gulf between Madhuri's back and all the others was the difference between the sun and moon. There was something about that back of Madhuri, its texture, build, and hue, that Aishwarya and the others just couldn't touch.

Rahul conducted a comparative study. The bodies of Gul Panag, Sushmita, Lara, and the rest of the newcomer starlets struck him as awfully artificial. Dieting, exercise, and everything else needed to maintain a model's figure had combined to produce bodies like plastic. On top of that, the hair waxing, expensive facials, spa treatments, and god knows what else. These creatures struck Rahul as nonhuman, synthetic dolls. From head to toe their hair didn't look quite real: even the light patch of underarm stubble seemed to him like artificial coloring. But it wouldn't take much—two weeks max. Feed them as humans, allow them to live as normal girls, and presto, their bellies would flab right out. You wouldn't even recognize them! But Madhuri? She was a species unto herself. Drop her into a slum, make her live in this hostel, feed her the fare of dal, rice, and oily vegetables we get in our mess hall, and even then, she wouldn't change a whit. She'd maintain the same miraculous radiance and the same dazzling beauty.

Madhuri's back was natural and authentic and, inexplicably, a swadeshi one. Made in India. The others were unnatural foreign imports and, Rahul deduced, that was the reason they held no charm. But far more momentous was his other conclusion, that girls took pleasure from pain, violence, and others' raw strength. And: girls preferred their sensual pleasure with a dash of humiliation, subjugation, and abuse. How times had changed. No one paid attention anymore to the '50s and '60s romantic film idol types like Shammi Kapoor, Rishi Kapoor, Vishwajeet, and Jitendra. Today's girls were crazy for the macho, sadistic sort like Salman Khan, Sunny Deol, and Ajay Devgan. How violent and menacing Shahrukh Khan had been in *Darr*, calling Juhi Chawla on the phone at all hours, stalking her, trying to rape her, finally stunning her into blood-soaked submission. She was so strangled with fear she could no longer speak. Yet it was this half-schizophrenic madman, Shahrukh Khan, who all the college girls went gaga over.

A Shahrukh: that's what the girls craved, not some kowtowing Krishnaesque pansy-brand husband. Rahul had unlocked the mystery, and since then Madhuri Dixit has been living in the window of Room 252. It's been four months.

TWO

Rahul had followed a peculiar career path. First he'd completed an MSc in organic chemistry. Afterward he suddenly became possessed with the idea of doing an MA in anthropology. The exact reasons for this are a bit fuzzy, but it might have had something to do with encouragement given to Rahul by a certain cousin of his, an internationally known anthropologist who nowadays was the director general of the Archaeological Survey of India. He used to visit Rahul's village, sometimes staying at his family house for a few weeks at a time. Rahul's father was his favorite uncle, and the two of them got along extremely well. The responsibility of looking after this cousin, Kinnu Da, fell to Rahul.

Rahul had heard that his book, published by Penguin, was about adivasis, tribals, and had caused a worldwide stir. Before the book came out, people assumed that it was only the usual cast of Brahmins, feudal landlords, business traders, Hindus, and Muslims that had been active in the fight against the British. Even contemporary historians selected their national heroes only among figures who came from these kinds of backgrounds. You could hardly find an adivasi or a Dalit untouchable in these historians' accounts, dominated by the likes of Laxmibai, Tatya Tope, another raja here, Nana Sahib, another landowner there, Kunwar Singh, Fadnavis, Azimullah, Mangal Pandey, or some nawab. Same back-

grounds, different names, when it came to twentieth-century leaders: Nehru, Gandhi, Tilak, Jinnah, Suhrawardy, Patel. Most of
them were of high caste and came from rich families. Once in a
blue moon Dr. Ambedkar's name might pop up. Although he came
from a Dalit caste, the man who would be called an untouchable
had been handed the task of framing the constitution of independent India as recognition of his singular genius. But now he's been
made the target of a smear campaign: sometimes accused of being
an agent of the English, other times portrayed as someone who
wanted to wipe out Hinduism in India in favor of establishing Bud-
dhism. In other words, more the story's villain than its hero.

Kinnu Da's book made such waves because, for the first time,
the story was told of the role of tribal adivasi leaders in the struggle.
Kinnu Da's book contained well-documented accounts from regions like Singhbhum and Jharkhand, including Chota Nagpur,
of leadership beset by great tragedy—accounts that had, until then,
existed only as living folklore in the underdeveloped regions of
Bihar, Bengal, and Orissa.

The more Kinnu Da spoke to Rahul, the more Rahul began to
suspect organic chemistry was a waste. What would he do with this
degree? He'd become a chemist in a brewery or in a food-processing
plant owned by some multinational company. Or he'd get a teaching
position at a college or university. When he thought about his future,
Rahul saw the image of a certain type of man take shape: fat, whiny,
gobbling pizza slices like a pig, gnawing on morsels of scrumptious
fish marinated in yogurt and vinegar, drinking and partying with a
teenage girl he was paying by the hour, enticing her with a little

dance of his by shaking his pot belly and gyrating his pumpkin-sized saggy ass.

This type of man—a bottomless pit of lust and greed, a decadent cheat, gluttonous, licentious, corrupt—that's who this country and system were set up to serve. All the shiny stores and legions of police and battalions of soldiers all exist to feed pleasure and stimulation to that man. If I work as an organic chemist, Rahul thought, I'll spend my whole life churning out yummy, lip-smacking, good-for-you consumables for *him*. This life, which the compassionate creator of the universe, acting with great kindness, has given, once and only once, to most negligible me.

Holy shit! The bastard is huffing and puffing, one foot dangling in the grave, he can't even walk right anymore he's so fat. But he keeps on chowing down. He needs a steady stream of edible items. His taste buds long for one new flavor after the next. Scientists the world over have conscripted lab after lab in order to research how to best please the man's palate. Each of the five senses that provide for his disgustingly doughy body require cutting-edge pleasures and never-ending kicks. His hippo-like snout eagerly sniffs for new fragrances and scents. The entire perfume industry exists in order to neutralize all malodors before they can reach his nose. If I work as an organic chemist, Rahul thought, the sum total of my creativity, talent, and knowledge will be pressed into service of satisfying the ever-growing appetite of this man's senses, and fulfilling the sensual desires of that libertine tub.

And this is the kind of man women everywhere are ripping their clothes off for. All the beauty parlors in the city lay the women down and wax their hair off, just as shepherds used to shear their sheep for wool. Rahul watched how herds of girls like little lambs came out from their middle- or lower-middle-class homes, in city after city, town after town, lunging into beauty parlors that were sprouting up like mushrooms. They'd reemerge: oiled, lubed, dolled up. Spreading their legs, they'd climb up and straddle that man's ample belly. These were the girls who on TV were called "the Bold and the Beautiful"; he was the flaccid, potbellied geezer known as "the Rich and the Famous."

The man was mighty indeed. The world's most fearsome evil masterminds had long labored to craft him from their toolkit of high-powered capital and patented processes. The introduction of new technologies was essential to his creation. We can only begin to guess at the super powers this man has at his disposal as we watch the true story of him take centuries' worth of theories, opinions, principles, philosophies, and ideas, all carefully crafted throughout history, sweep them into a pile and, in one fell swoop, throw it onto the trash heap that lies just beyond the walls of his stately manor. Those were the principles used both as a kick when man needed a nudge to move forward, but also as the reins that kept his greed and lust from spiraling out of control.

Don't eat more than you need, don't make more money than necessary, do as little harm as possible, don't sleep too much, sex has a limit, don't dance forever. All of these principles, found in religious texts and in sociological, scientific, and political books, have been tossed wholesale into the rubbish. In the final decades of the twentieth century, this man has seized all the forces of wealth and power and technology into his hand and has declared: freedom! Freedom! he cries. Let all your desires be awakened! Let all your senses graze freely upon this earth. Whatever is in this world is yours for your enjoyment. There is neither nation nor country. The entire planet is yours. Nothing is moral, nothing is immoral. There is no sin, no act of virtue. Eat, drink, and have fun. Dance! Boogie-woogie. Sing! Boogie-woogie. Eat! Boogie-woogie. Pig out! Boogie-woogie. Make that six-figure salary! Boogie-woogie. All the earth's commodities are yours for your consumption! Boogie-woogie. And remember to count women among those commodities. Boogie-woogie.

This mighty, swinish, lustful man proposed a new doctrine that the finance minister of India readily agreed to—and then the minister himself eagerly dove into the man's pocket. Here was the principle: don't stop the man from eating. As he eats and eats and begins to get full, he starts to flick off the spoiled morsels from his plate. Millions of hungry people could be fed with his rich, nutritious leftovers. And: don't stop the man from fucking. Popping Viagra like candy, the man beds one girl after the next, readying them for the legions of unwitting Indian bachelors who, duped into believing they have landed a virgin, can then love her as their own, and start a family.

So this was the principle the man spread to the four corners of the earth using all media of communication, and in no time at all human civilization had changed. Every TV channel and computer buzzed with the broadcast of this philosophy.

Here, at the twilight of the twentieth century and the dawn of the twenty-first, even names like Gandhi, Tolstoy, Premchand, and Tagore have begun to disappear from people's memories. The best-selling book in stores today? *The Road Ahead*, by Bill Gates.

The rich, potbellied man was getting a massage in an expensive island resort, surrounded by several Miss Universes from the destitute third world. Remembering something, he suddenly reached for his cell phone and dialed a number.

Miss Universe slipped him a Viagra—which he quickly swallowed—and then he gave her breast a little squeeze.

"Hallo! This is Nikhlani speaking on behalf of the IMF. Get me to the prime minister!"

"Yes, yes! Nikhlani-ji! How are you, sir? This is the prime minister speaking."

"Stroke it gently . . . rub it a bit more! Oh, that's more like it," that man said, sweetly teasing Miss Universe, and then returned to his cell phone. "Why have you taken so long, man? Hurry up! The power sector, IT, Food, Health, Education! Hurry up and privatize! Divest the public sector!"

"Okay, Okay, be patient. Your humble servant is doing his duty. But you know my problem. In this hodge-podge government, you can't expect all of the dal to soften at once, Nikhlani-ji."

"Take it in your mouth . . . Lo . . . my Lolita." The Rich and the Famous geezer stroked Miss Universe's hair, and this was followed by the sounds of slurping.

"I'm disappointed, Pandit-ji! How much money did I pump into your party funds? The donations, the direct deposits! You people move as fast as a dirty earthworm. How we gonna fix the economy at this rate? You haven't even cut subsidies!"

"It is going forward, Nikhlani-ji! I've already begun the food-oil importation that wiped out the sunflower, soybean, and oilseed farmers. If we took away their subsidies now, all hell would break loose. Your instructions are being carried out, don't worry. We're just taking one step at a time."

"Hurry up, Pandit-ji! I've got high blood pressure. This much anxiety isn't good for my health. Let those sisterfucking farmers starve. Okay?"

The man switched off his cell phone and took a long pull of scotch. Then, again restless, he said, "Where's that runner-up from Venezuela? Send her in."

THREE

Kinnu Da addressed Rahul. "The most significant thing about the adivasis is that they have so few needs. They leave a minimal mark on the environment. I've documented adivasi communities in Singhbhum, Jharkhand, Mayurbhanj, Bastar, and the Northeast that still practice slash-and-burn agriculture and confine themselves to raw, roasted, or boiled foods. They won't even fry their food. This is a kind of natural way of living. But keep in mind, they fought like hell against the British for their autonomy, their right to self-rule. But historians never included that chapter in their versions of history. The truth is that history is a highly political record of power. The class, caste, or ethnic group on top will fashion history to suit their needs. I've always said that the history of this indigenous state and its people remains to be written."

Rahul was afraid. Just a few days back he'd seen a film called *Stigmata.* God's messenger shall be silenced. Truth and information are two different things. Truth is like a bomb to the information industry. Therefore, the truth must be neutralized.

Whoosh; *plunk*. A leaf falls.

Plunk. Full of its own nectar, a pure fruit falls silently to the ground, prematurely, in a desolate place.

Plunk. Another murder will be committed, or suicide; a paragraph's mention, buried in the back of tomorrow's paper.

Plunk-plunk-plunk-plunk! Time passes. The earth spins on its axis.

Kinnu Da was transferred time and again from one adivasi region to the next. *He's crazy, a real nutcase*—that's how his colleagues in the civil service talked about him behind his back. *All that time in government service, and, except for his pension, he's broke. He can barely afford a flat in Delhi.*

Rahul began to sour on organic chemistry, which started to smell of the stench of vinegar and fermentation. The very name was like an airtight chamber filled with the farts and belches of the fat man.

So I'll do an MA in anthropology instead, Rahul thought, and then a PhD. And I will endeavor to reach the root of this problem known as mankind. O supreme one! Give me the strength and faith to discover how Satan managed to sabotage history for his own benefit!

But what about Madhuri Dixit? And her backside? And her startled doe-like eyes?

Rahul crumpled a piece of paper into a ball, loaded it into the slingshot, and drew it back as far as he could. *Pfffff!* The paper ball whizzed through the air and hit Madhuri Dixit right on the bottom.

"Oooooooh!" came her sweet voice, soaked in music and infused with quivering pain. The doe turned her head and looked lovingly at her hunter. "Thank you, Rahul! Thank you for the boo-boo! I love you!"

FOUR

It was the second month after the beginning of the term. The university was known as "the Cambridge of India" and it spread over a few hundred acres surrounded by mountains scattering far into the distance. Students came here from Japan, Indonesia, Fiji, Mauritius, and even from a few African countries. The chair of the geology department was the world-famous Professor Watson. He'd turned down offers from all the major academic institutions in the U.S., France, and Germany in favor of India, since the astonishing variety of what he found here was better for his research. "This country is a living museum of wonders. Countless cultures, histories, races, and castes . . . We've found evidence of human civilization here from as long ago as several hundred thousand years: alive, robust, burning brightly. And what applies to people equally applies to the ground we're standing on."

Dr. Watson went on. Bending over, he picked up a rock, which he examined with great care. "Look at this. This rock reveals the lava stage of the mountain on which this university was established. Look carefully. It's actually a fossil, a thousand years old, maybe a hundred thousand. And it's the fossil of some aquatic life. Right where we're standing now, on this very spot, there once was an ocean."

The people standing around suddenly looked confused. An ocean? Here? In Madhya Pradesh?

Rahul began to enjoy himself. He'd been assigned to the second floor of Tagore Hostel, Room 252, with a roommate, O.P., Omkar Prasad. O.P. was six foot three, thin like a bamboo stick, neck like a heron's, bobbing at every step. O.P. was a clown and a chatterbox and declared, "I'll marry a four-foot maiden. It'll give these mountain people something to stare at when we make love in the 'standing position.'"

Rahul pictured himself strolling in town in the shadow of the mountain. Looking up at the sky, he admires the full moon, shining like a golden plate in the night. His gaze wanders over the peak of the highest mountain where he notices a gigantic man, naked as Adam. Rahul makes out an impish apparition, like a tiny woman, fastened to the giant's waist, and then the wind carries a thump to Rahul's ears—a sound like someone drumming on an hourglass-shaped damaru. Thump! Thump! Thump! The figures sway back and forth. Who are they? O.P. and his fantasy girl? Or the maiden of the rock? The daughter of the Himalayas? It's Shiva and Parvati! So this was the cosmic union from which the world was created. Thump! Thump! Thump!

Father used to get up at half past four every morning, bathe, then perform puja to Shiva. Sometimes the Sanskrit chanting and echoing of the prayer through the house woke Rahul in the silence of the dawn:

namami shamisham nirvana vibhum, vibhuam vyapakam
    bahma ved swarupam
ajum nirgunam nirvikalpam niriham, cidahashamahasha
    vasam bhajeham
nirankara monkara mulam turiyam

FIVE

O.P. proved to be a very good friend. To meet his expenses, Rahul was forced to tutor two students—which none other than O.P. had arranged. He'd been studying at the university for two years, had already completed his MSc in criminology, and was now doing advanced research. O.P. didn't need to worry about funds, since he was receiving a prestigious UGC—University Grants Commission—scholarship.

Rahul discovered that the very contours of the university were changing fast. In the past few years, foreign students had stopped applying. Internationally renowned thinkers like Dr. Watson wanted out, and were putting out feelers elsewhere. The situation was deteriorating.

He heard about the female student from Mauritius who'd been abducted last year by some goondas who raped and killed her. The thugs threw her body into a ditch under a footbridge. O.P. warned Rahul, "You'd better be careful and keep your wits about you. If you go into town, don't look for trouble. Even if you're just buying a ticket at the cinema, don't flash a 100- or 500-rupee note, because it's not just the guy sitting in the booking window you have to worry about. It's everyone. The paan seller and the chaat vendor, they're all in on the racket. If they suspect you're the kid of some Assamese high roller, they'll come by the

hostel whenever they feel like it and take you away. Every year you hear about dozens of abductions. This is an old dacoit stomping ground. Devi Singh, Malkhan Singh, Mohar Singh, Tahsildar Singh—that whole gang of dacoits used to prowl around here and wreak havoc."

Rahul soon realized O.P. was telling the truth. Even the postman was in cahoots with the goondas. Money orders from families of South Indian students or others who were a long way from home usually arrived on the first of the month. The goondas knew precisely how much each student received. As soon as the clock struck nine thirty on the night of money-order day, a couple of jeeps would pull up to the hostel. Out they'd come wielding hockey sticks, cycle chains, iron rods, homemade pistols, any weapons they could easily get their hands on cheap from the local mechanic. They addressed one another with goofy nicknames like Ajju, Lacchu, Acchan, Babban, Cuppy, Penda, Guddu, Dabba, Boxy. To denote rank and seniority they'd add "Little Brother," "Elder Brother," or "Guru." So there'd be Acchan Guru or Brother Lacchu. Every so often someone would even achieve the rank of Ustad: Parasu Ustad, for example. Of course, these characters were connected to local politicians and police, but on top of this they also wielded considerable influence both in student politics and within the university administration. The goondas called students who came from Assam, Manipur, or Arunachal "monkeys" or "mallu"; South Indians or students from other countries were "rundu."

A Manipuri student named Sapam Tomba lived in Room 212. He was handsome, pleasantly plump, a quick student, and a good badminton player. He and Rahul had gotten to know each other well. Sapam was in his first year of an MSc in botany. A couple of weeks ago, at home near Imphal, his older brother, a primary school teacher, had been killed by gunfire. Sapam cried and cried. He couldn't go back to Manipur to attend his brother's funeral: first because he didn't have enough money for the trip, and second because his father forbade him to return home. Incidents related to the insurgency in Manipur were on the rise, and the whole state was overrun with the Indian Army and Border Security Force personnel that executed "combing operations" and had deadly "encounters" with insurgents every day. "If I go home, they'll say I am a PLA member and shoot me. It's safer here than there," Sapam said.

The goondas had broken into Sapam's room, too. They took his watch, 600 rupees from a money order, a teakettle, and a thermos. But that wasn't the worst of it. They made Sapam strip naked and tried to force him to pee on the hot electric heater. They tortured him until he gave in; Sapam passed out cold from the electric shock. He still hadn't returned to a state that could be called normal; they had broken him. He'd cry and ask, "Where can I go? How can I continue with my studies? Tell me!"

O.P., Rahul, and a few other students pitched in to pay Sapam's mess bill and school fees. "Manipuri people want to separate from India. If an election were held today, the number of Manipuris and Nagas voting for the separatists would exceed even the numbers in Kashmir who want independence."

How did this happen?

Sapam said that many women in Manipur who had become widows, including his own aunt, go to Brindavan, home of Krishna.

The famous Ras Lila, performed in honor of Krishna, was now staged in villages all over Manipur, and the festivals included devotional hymns in praise of Krishna. In the seventeenth century, Gaurang Mahaprabhu Chaitanya spread his devotional poetry and songs from Bengal until they echoed throughout Manipur. The result was that all of the people, including adivasis, became Vaishnavas, devotees of Krishna. These simple, sweet, straightforward, thoughtful people, living the difficult life of the mountains, Mongol or Tibeto-Burmese Meiteis and adivasis, attached surnames like Sharma and Singh to their names. As if Chaitanya had flooded their spiritually barren souls with a torrent of salubrious nectar. In 1947, after partition, Manipur held a referendum and by the will of its people decided to join the Republic of India.

So why has it come to this? Within fifty years, why do 99 percent of the people want independence from India?

Sapam spoke: "The Mayang foreigners looted everything. They took our girls. They humiliated us. The market, trade, employment —Mayang controlled everything. If you even opened your mouth, you'd be labeled a separatist. If the army leaves Manipur, there'll be independence the next day." He continued, "During the British time, we gave our blood to Subhash Bose's Indian National Army. We fought for India's independence all the way to Burma. Now we'll fight for our own independence. Mark my words: we'll be free from India before Kashmir is."

Rahul decided that university life wasn't as easy as he first thought. First you had to worry about personal safety, and after that the studying all the time, reading thick anthropology books, trying to get to the root of mankind and civilization, and gazing at Madhuri

Dixit's backside. It was no walk in the park. The local goondas could break in at any moment and put a gun to your head. We are merely prey living in a cruel, criminal, and degrading time. It's an age of thugs, counterfeiters, smugglers, and real-estate developers. Nowadays, righteous and upstanding Indians suffer under this regime as if they were Kashmiris, Manipuris, or Naxalites.

Kinnu Da explained, "Last month I was invited to take part in a seminar in New York. I had the minimum 500 dollars with me. I'd never brought more cash than that, because I don't spend it. But this time, for the first time, they questioned me. I was asked very rudely, 'How are you going to get by with this? Why didn't you bring more with you?'" Kinnu Da continued, "The truth is the world now belongs to businessmen. They bring hundreds of thousands of dollars with them when they travel. Transactions worth billions are traded. They can't fathom that there are still some people left in India who don't crave making a fortune, and who travel to America or France not to do business but for academic or other reasons."

So globalization exists only for those who are players in the global market: speculators, bootleggers, government ministers, and bureaucrats. Suppose someone like the humanitarian Dr. Kotnis wanted to go to China nowadays, or someone like the Communist agitator Tibeto-Buddhologist monk Mahapandit Rahul Sankrityayan wanted to go to Russia or Central Asia. Would it be possible?

"Not at all!" said Kartikeya. "This is the end of the civil society. It's vanished from everywhere. Only governments, companies, institutions, the Mafia, and interest groups remain. If, by chance, you happen to see some writer, poet, or thinker sitting on a plane taking a trip abroad, you can be sure that he's just a middleman or lackey, secretly on the take, working for some company, institution, or corporation. *Always doubt his integrity!*"

Kartikeya Kajle was from Pune. Alongside doing research in geology, he was getting ready to take the civil service exam. He told Rahul that he, too, should give it a try.

After Sapam, the goondas went after Madhusudan, a student from Kerala, who was beaten so badly and got so scared that he jumped from the second floor and broke his legs. Rahul, O.P., and Kartikeya went to the hospital to visit him. His father had written him a telegram instructing him to apply for an academic transfer and return to Cochin at once. Madhusudan was distraught. His entire future was ruined.

One day Rahul, along with Anima, Abha, Deepti, Manmohan, and Raju, was headed from his department to the canteen near the library. There was a group of six or seven boys hanging out by the side of the road, and one of them threw a rock that hit Rahul on the back of the head. Anima shrieked. There was no blood. One of them shouted, "Hey, big hero! Nice hair. That sweet little part in the middle, just like Rahul Ray."

"You're all a bunch of loudmouths," Anima scolded.

"Hey, big sis. You bringing that little girlie man home to meet our momma? Why don't you go look for a real boy instead?" They burst into hysterical laughter.

"We should end this right here. Be quiet and keep walking," Manmohan advised.

So they kept going. It seemed the worst had passed. But as soon as they turned the corner to the canteen, another rock whizzed past and hit Abha in the head. She cried out and fell down. Her glasses broke and blood streamed from her forehead.

"Did you come to this school to study or chase skirts? This is our first warning. Watch yourself, hero. Otherwise we'll set your clock straight." From behind came another voice from among them. "And go fuck your baoo!"

"Baoo" means mother.

They went to the proctor's office to lodge a complaint. This much bullying and abuse was unimaginable. Abha went to the dispensary to have her wound dressed. She couldn't see without her glasses. And on top of everything else, finals were looming.

Dr. Chaturvedi was the proctor. He listened to the whole story while using a toothpick to dig at bits of supari caught in his teeth. Then he sat up straight and said in a serious yet shrewd tone of voice, "Look, this isn't Delhi or London. If you go around having your jollies with modern girls, fashion girls, well, something's bound to happen. Everyone's eyeing these girls. The teachers aren't far behind the students on this count. Today you got a rock thrown at you. Tomorrow you'll flunk your courses."

"But, sir! We weren't having that kind of fun at all. We were just going to the canteen before our next period for some refreshments, sir," Rahul countered.

"Oh? And where have you come from, Mr. Smarty-pants? And why do you part your hair in the middle like that? Is that what girls go for nowadays?" Proctor Chaturvedi said sarcastically. "Look, mister, if making friends with girls is such a big hobby of yours, then at least find some money to put in your pocket. Get a car. Why risk walking around so openly with them? All these cars with their tinted windows I see driving on campus from town, who knows what's going on inside? C'mon, there are hotels every-where—why don't you try one of them? If you keep on like this, it'll be dangerous not just for you, but for the girls. It's a poisonous atmosphere here. In no time at all, you'll have nonsense scrawled all over the walls on campus. It's nothing to you, but what happens to the poor maiden whose name's been dragged through mud then left high and dry?"

"Sir, you are misunderstanding, sir." Manmohan whimpered.

"It's not me who is misunderstanding, it's you," Chaturvedi said, now done picking his teeth. "Your minds have gone bad from watching too much TV. Focus on your studies. And about today's little incident: what should I do, summon the deputy of police? Go ahead and press charges. By all means. But don't forget that these boys are locals. They pelted you on the head with a rock today only to give you a warning. They were taunting you. Tomorrow they'll break into your hostel and beat you like there's no tomorrow. My advice for you people? Return to your department, nice and quiet, and don't wander around in groups like that anymore."

They left. The pain in Abha's head was getting worse. Rahul felt the back of his own head swelling up a bit.

So this was the postmodern age when, thanks to ads on TV, Valentine's Day was celebrated in small towns, and even in the roughest, most backward neighborhoods, the demand for choco-late cake and Archie's greetings cards for New Year's was on the rise.

Watch the shorn-headed ascetic caveman drink Pepsi and breakdance in front of the Ram temple, cheap pistol fastened to phallus. And see his sack filled with dirty money laundered by Ibrahim, criminal don, living in Dubai.

Vote for him—he'll bring on the Hindu Raj.

The swelling on Rahul's head began to throb. What if the blood wasn't clotting properly? He was scared.

SIX

Around two thirty that afternoon, it happened to Rahul: the event that takes place for some only once in a lifetime.

There were a few clouds in the sky; it had rained two days before. All the trees and buildings on campus, freshly washed by the rain, sparkled in the midday sun.

The color of August is a lush, deep green, and the days are filled with the earthy fragrance of wet grass. Going for a walk in August means having your shoes muddied with blades of grass or tender shoots. It's the season for eating roasted corn on the cob.

After the stone-throwing incident, Rahul and his friends went on alert. The day when Rahul's life changed forever, he sat with his friends in the department common room: Abha, Seema Philip, Manmohan, Rana, Anima, Raju, Renu, Neera Didi, and Bhagvat. They ate their corn on the cob, started playing Hindi film song games, then argued about cricket and TV series, and wound up playing the table like a tabla and taking turns singing songs. They'd bolted the windows and doors from the inside to be sure none of the local goondas would barge in and cause trouble. It was two days until the holiday of Rakshabandhan, when sisters tie colorful threads of affection—the rakhi—around the wrists of their brothers, or those they consider like brothers. Talk was thick about which girls, by dint of tying the rakhi around the wrist of a boy or a teacher, would cancel once and for all the one-sided soap opera and recast the once-aspiring lover as esteemed brother. Raju and Neera Didi had in their possession a bona fide treasure trove of juicy information.

Neera Didi began. "So Aggrawal Sir is always coming to campus these days wearing this cap. The other day it started raining and the cap got totally soaked. Water ran through it like an old rag. But he still refused to take it off. He didn't want Rita Saxena to see his bald head and go run off with someone else."

"If a girl sits on Aggrawal's head, she'll slip and she'll fall and she might wind up dead!" Raju rhymed along with his tabla-like drumming on the table.

"And then there's that Hindi poet, Tiwari Sir. I heard the other day that the librarian told him off in front of everyone. She asked him, 'Do you come to the library to look at the books, or to ogle the girls?'"

"He's a Peeping Tom and a voyeur! They say he even called the parents of girls to tattle on them. He got beaten up for it once."

"The jerk even won the Padmashree award. He's a great big slimy leech. Now he's in London at the behest of the World Hindi Conference."

That day Anima was wearing a plum-colored sleeveless blouse and a sea-blue silk sari. It went with her dusky complexion and gave her some pizzazz. Her pimply, flat face had a mischievous twinkle like a kid's, but her eyes were big and innocent. She sang:

Oh love of my youth, please don't leave my heart
When you think of me, please pray we'll never part

and then

Our love is perfect, lover, so strong it will not break
He who puts me to the test should come with ring and cake

Anima's voice was like a sorrowful flute whose notes didn't project outward but rather inward, descending somewhere deep inside. Her voice affected Raju, who nearly fell into a trance with his drumming. What sadness must there be inside of this dark girl to make her voice well up so?

Abha sang a rap song she'd written herself. It was a riot. Rahul pitched in with a Panjabi pop song of Hansraj: *Hey, pretty girl, don't walk alone, come on with me, let's leave this world behind.*

The song was so catchy that soon Rana, Neera Didi, Abha, Anima, and the rest joined in.

"How about some Daler Mendhi?" Raju requested. Everyone sang along.

Just then someone knocked on the door.

The tabla reverted once again to a mute, wooden table as silence spread through the room. At this hour? Who could it be? All the teachers were off at the vice-chancellor's residence and wouldn't be back until five in the evening.

Could it be some gang member? In their singing reverie they'd forgotten that their voices probably carried into the corridor.

Rahul went to the door and unlatched it.

And there she was, standing at the door. She, whom Rahul saw for the first time in his whole life.

Here were her two big eyes brimming with surprise. On the brink of laughter, her lips and cute little nose suddenly frozen. She wore a Jaipuri tie-dyed green, yellow-and-red-spotted chunni. Her kurta was the yellow of spring flowers and her salwar was white. She was very fair skinned, with a drop of honey brown.

"Hi, Anjali!" Seema Philip and Anima called out.

"What are you guys up to? I didn't disturb anything, did I?' Anjali asked, sitting down next to Anima.

"No, yaar, you just logged on to www.time-pass-musical.com," Seema said.

"Do you want some corn on the cob? I've got half of mine left," offered Renu.

"Heaven forbid! She's a strict Brahmin," Seema said in jest. "She'll become an outcaste if she eats your defiled piece of food."

Anjali began to munch on the corn. Rahul watched her. How could a girl look so beautiful, so innocent, so vulnerable?

Rahul felt as if a cool, peaceful breeze had entered the room with Anjali.

Chappa, chappa charkha chale, awni bawni bereyon tale . . .

Raju picked up the tempo on the table. Then, in a soft, slow voice, Rana began singing again. Rahul joined in here and there.

It turned out that Anjali was the daughter of Joshi, a cabinet minister at the state level. L. K. Joshi, minister of the Public Works Department. The family must have come from the hills once upon a time, but they'd been living in town for generations. Joshi had started as a forest contractor and then became a real-estate developer. He'd made millions. During this round of elections, his first time running for office, Joshi got on the ticket for the state legislature, won, and then finagled a state ministerial appointment. Behind him was the full weight of the businessmen, contractors, and real-estate dealers. He could also count on such criminal characters as Acchan, Bablu, and Lakhan Pandey.

Joshi was considered one better than the Machiavellian political sage Chanakya, or so was common belief in the area. People said one day he'd go far in national politics. Astrologers clearly saw that it was in the stars.

And Anjali? That girl munching merrily away on her corn on the cob?

Anjali was the girlfriend of Seema Philip and Anima. The three of them had gone to the same inter-college for girls and had been inseparable. Anima said that Anjali was doing her MA in Hindi.

An MA in Hindi?

Rahul did a double take. An image of the Hindi department flashed before his eyes: the dull, gray, sick-looking walls, the red stains from paan juice spat out, garbage strewn in the corners, filth everywhere. It was as if the most isolated part of the university had been plunged into a blighted darkness. The mysterious building was serving a life sentence in solitary confinement.

And the people who went in and out of the department! They didn't look like they were living in today's world. From the clothes they wore to the way they walked and talked, they were completely *other*. The males often traveled around campus together in a pack. Girls would see them and take fright. They spoke in high-pitched voices, screeching loudly, clapping their hands, having a coughing fit, all the while laughing at their own jokes in a sound like that of a mirthful primal man who'd jumped the fence into civilization. Ha-ha, hee-hee, hoo-hoo.

They were at once ridiculous and frightful, inspiring both pity and fear. They spoke in a peculiar language among themselves, some spirit tongue of a dead culture.

Hindi, Urdu, Sanskrit: nobody really knew for sure why these three departments existed at all. What kind of future would their graduates have? No one had a clue. Those boys were ragged, misfits, backward, isolated from the real world, and their teachers made for the same caricature. One student would shamelessly scratch his crotch in public, while another shaved-head dhoti-clad type would ogle some girl like a chimpanzee.

Students on campus jokingly referred to the department as "leftover land." Any girl with brains and talent took admission in any of the other departments that were part of the university mainstream. Only the leftovers enrolled in the Hindi department. One look at them and you knew: *dropouts*.

Could this Anjali Joshi really be part of that same Hindi department? What if next week she turns into a mother gorilla? She'll look like some forest-dwelling rishi chick, speaking in middle Indo-Aryan or Pali, smeared with turmeric paste, drinking boiled cow or yak's milk. Rahul heard from Anima that Anjali had been quite ill around the time of her graduation. She'd come down with jaundice, and was in a miserable state when she took her exams. Her grades, understandably, were simply awful, and she barely passed. So her father had a word with S. N. Mishra, the head of the Hindi department, who took care of matters, and so she was admitted.

Kinnu Da once said, "Take any language. As long as there is some group of people, somewhere, using it to communicate, it won't vanish. In spite of the massive spread of European languages, centuries of colonialism and imperialist subjugation, the itsy-bitsy indigenous languages of Africa and Asia still haven't been eradicated. Living languages still exist today, like Ho, which is spoken by only a few adivasis."

So, they are the tribals! They are the adivasis of today.

"No, those aren't the adivasis," Kartikeya countered. "They're the Muslim mullahs and the Hindu purohits. Don't forget, an adivasi is never retrogressive. He adapts to the times."

I'll become a gorilla, too. A homo sapiens. A purohit. I'll chew paan and gutkha, run around in a pack and laugh and laugh: *Ha-ha, hee-hee, hoo-hoo.*

Rahul watched from the corridor. In between Anima and Seema Philip was Anjali Joshi, walking away. In her right hand she held a parasol. A yellow parasol.

He had no doubt it was the same back that deflected the sun's rays from Room 252. "If I had a slingshot," Rahul thought, "I'd pull the rubber band all the way back to my ear and let loose a shot."

A voice drenched in song, gratitude, and bittersweet pain would moan "Oooooooh," and she would turn around with stunned, eager, inviting eyes.

And she would freeze in that pose.

That day was truly the first time in Rahul's life that a real, living, breathing, flesh-and-blood girl had been captured in a freeze-frame, and her name was Anjali Joshi.

SEVEN

The emergency session took place at nine o'clock p.m., after dinner, on the field below Tagore Hostel. Nearly all of the boys from Maharshi Arvind, CV Raman, and Bhulabhai Desai hostels came out. There were also two other hostels: MLB (Maharani Laxmibai) and Sarojini Naidu Girls' Hostel. Parvez and Kannan had sent the word over to them, and soon enough forty-five girls showed up.

"Death to Vice-Chancellor Agnihotri!"

"Shame on Chaturvedi!"

"Warden Upadhyay: come out, come out, wherever you are!"

"Comrades! Today we have come together as one to sort out some very serious business. If we don't rise up today, we're finished. This university's become a haven for goondas and antisocial criminal elements. They do whatever they feel like and right out in the open. Your fellow students who stand among you now will tell you what the goondas did to them. I'll start with the resident of Tagore Hostel, Room 212, Sapam Tomba, who came here to study from Manipur and is in his first-year MSc."

Sapam made his way to the dais and in broken Hindi and English began to tell the story of the calamity that befell him. In the middle, he choked up and began to weep right on stage. Maybe it was the sight of so many students, or his state of raw emotion, or his anxiety—but it was the first time he'd told the story to anyone. He'd even kept it hidden from the university administration.

In the middle of his jerky sobs, as Sapam described the excesses he suffered at the hands of the goondas, he stopped for an instant, eyes seeming to stray off into space and fix on nothing in particular, and then, covering his eyes, he let it all out in one big breath. "Before forcing me to piss on the electric heater, they tried to sodomize me." This was too much; he utterly fell apart. A new flood of tears breached his hands and drenched his face.

It was as if a majestic bird, flapping its wounded wings, had fallen suddenly into the middle of the crowd. A frightful silence spread, and everyone stood still. The faces of the students gathered on the field below Tagore Hostel were covered with the grit of sorrow, disgust, defeat, and shame. An unbearable, soul-raking silence filled the ears of everyone present. And from the stage came Sapam Tomba's sobbing voice.

"I am not a gay," he said in English. "Tell me, how can I go on? Why should I even try?" Sapam's crying was now like a typhoon, once held back, now let loose. His delicate, lovely body trembled like a frail plant in a swiftly moving storm. Only a few days ago his brother, a primary school teacher, had been gunned down in Manipur, while here, Sapam had endured this.

"Every day I think about suicide. And . . . I'll definitely do it! Mark my words. If not today, then tomorrow. Why go on living? My brother sent me money so I could study. Now who will pay the bills? Tell me. Tell me!"

Everyone's eyes were moist with tears. You could hear the sound of girls' sobbing.

Rahul went up to Sapam and placed a hand on his shoulder. He himself was having a hard time holding it together. With great difficulty, he cleared his throat and said, "Come, come. Come down here, Sapam. It's enough. You can hold it together." Sapam's red, swollen eyes glanced at Rahul, and, slowly balancing himself on him for support, Sapam began to descend the steps of the platform.

The meeting lasted until midnight. It was concluded that either the security arrangements at the university were insufficient or, because of the presence of certain locals, no steps had been taken to fight the criminals. The administration acted this way maybe out of fear, or maybe an ulterior motive lurked behind. Who could say? Aside from Sapam, a few others came forward to speak—Madhusudan, Praveen, Niketan, and Masood—who'd also been beaten and had money and belongings stolen this term at the hands of the goondas. Pratap Parihar, whose uncle was a police officer, said these goondas had secured protection from police, university officials, and politicians. Last year, a senior named Jay Prakash Bhuiyan filed a complaint with the police against the goondas, naming them by name. A few months later, as he was waiting at the train station to go back home to his village, the goondas caught up with him on the platform and beat him up in front of the railway police, breaking both his hands. Afterward, he was forced to drop out of school.

It was decided that all the students living in the hostels would unite to take on the goondas.

"Don't assume they've locked up support from all of the local students. We've talked with the 'day scholars,' and they're with us.

Sure, they come from the same place and know all the same people, so, okay, they might not support us openly. But they'll find some other ways to help us."

"Believe me when I tell you that these goondas are few in number. Their strength and boldness have shot up only because of their weapons and political connections. If we let them know what we're made of, loud and clear, they'll think twice before breaking into our hostels again."

Pratap Parihar's and Kartikeya's speeches were powerful.

It was also decided that the next time such an incident happened, the students would shut down the whole university.

Strike! Strike! Long live student unity!

The meeting was forceful and a complete success. Rahul felt as if the blood in his veins had suddenly picked up speed and was being licked by flames. He gazed at his biceps. The trips to the gym looked like they were paying off. *I belong to a martial race. I will fight for a just cause till I breathe my last.*

He slowly began to hum. "I shall live and die for you, O Motherland . . . I gave you my heart and I shall give you my life, O Motherland . . ." He gently squeezed Sapam's shoulder and gave him a smile.

But Sapam didn't return his smile. His eyes wandered off, lost in empty space. What was there? Was it his dead brother, who could only watch Sapam with his sad, helpless, lifeless eyes, and do nothing? He'd been shot. Blood still flowed from his temple. Sapam saw him right there, sitting quietly in the corner of the field below Tagore Hostel, looking at Sapam with his dead eyes.

Every morning, he'd hoist his younger brother Sapam onto

the bicycle, take the net, and go catch fish. At home ducks ran everywhere. Behind their house was dense forest, and mountains, whose color changed all day because of the sun's and clouds' continual play of light and shade. Mountains that appeared blue in morning would look gray or brown as afternoon crept along; then, a sudden shadow from a cloud falling on the mountain, and it transformed completely, green. It was a wonderful sight to watch the mountains disappear right before your very eyes, totally, without a trace. Only the fog of the clouds, suspended to the side of the mountain, was left to see. His brother used to tell him, "That's how plane crashes happen, Sapam. The pilot thinks it's just fog when really there's a big mountain ahead."

In the summer heat, the thick, wet bamboo stands in the forest became dry, and when the evening wind blew swiftly through the stalks, they droned as if a thousand bansuris played. Father said that when Krishna fell in love with Rukmini, the sound from his flute floated through this same bamboo forest. Rukmini was from right here, the Northeast. These bamboo learned how to play the bansuri from Krishna. Even today, Rukmini comes to the jungle to meet Krishna, secretly disguised as the wind.

Sapam's father drummed on the dholak during the devotional kirtan songs. He played very well, and so totally submerged himself in the singing and drumming that people said the spirit of Chaitanya had entered into him. Chaitanya, the great master!

Sapam had turned into a stone statue.

It gave Rahul a shudder. Then he found his friend and roommate, O.P., six foot three, himself a bamboo stick, with a neck as long and delicate as a swan or heron's, bobbing at every step, standing straight up in the middle of the crowd. His thin, oval face was burning with rage.

Rahul came up quietly to O.P. and hugged him from behind. "Hey, Guinness book contender, why aren't you looking around for your petite girl? There must be one here somewhere in this crowd. Forget about fighting the goondas. And if by chance your girl did show up, your great house of bones would break in ten places."

"Shut up! This is no time for jokes," O.P. fumed. But as Rahul tightened his grip and twisted harder O.P. began to laugh amid his wincing. "Uncle! Uncle! Okay, you win!"

EIGHT

The SMTF—Special Militant Task Force—consisted of twenty-five young men. Pratap Parihar had not only procured iron rods, khurkhuri blades, Rampuri knives, hockey sticks, tiger's claws, cycle chains, billy clubs, and lathi sticks, but also arranged for three makeshift pistols.

Rahul and Madhusudan lifted the recipe for Molotov cocktails from Che Guevara's *Venceremos* and filled ten soda bottles with gasoline, caustic soda, and miscellaneous shrapnel. Sapam and Kartikeya crafted homemade hand grenades from gunpowder, potash, lead shot, shards of glass, and nails that, when thrown, would burst open and cause all hell to break loose. These were the weapons for tossing into jeeps from the roof of the hostel, should the goondas happen to come at night.

"Venceremos! Venceremos! We shall overcome—we shall overcome! Our hearts are filled with faith!"

After that night, hostel warden Chandramani Upadhyay would seem like a scared, worried little mouse. Just over the last few days, he'd noticed a clear change in the boys' behavior. The Namaste Index had fallen off sharply, went into a downward spiral, and nearly crashed. Even the rare "namaste" delivered like a blood-sucking protégé, reminiscent of the golden age and good old days, came from the lips of either a student from his department or a real ass kisser. Upadhyay had an eagle eye, infallible, for spotting boys of his own caste; so how was it he was now being fooled by not recognizing his own kind? Before, when he walked the halls, students made way and greeted him with a "namaste" or "adab" as he went by. Now they stood in groups, looked at him like he was some weird insect, and walked past talking among themselves, ignoring him. So now he stuck to the edge of the hallway. He was scared. Who knew if one of those bastards might take a cheap shot?

It's been said the age of information and technology had descended upon India, and on Delhi, and then somehow even got dragged all the way to this university. Students had in their possession reams of information about each and every person. Only a short distance from the hostel complex a "Max Cyber Cafe" opened where a few boys made what they called "de facto" files on professors and administrators. Hemant Barua, a student from Assam studying in the Department of Mathematics (and simultaneously working on an e-commerce degree from the private IT school NIIT), led the information-gathering effort. Hemant was a chess master and his number-crunching skills were dumbfounding. He was short and dark, his hair curly, his eyes tiny, smiling, and blinking. Every day Hemant and Rahul played chess for an hour or so. When Rahul confessed his crush on Anjali, Hemant said, "Hold on a little while. First I'll put together a full profile on the girl."

Meanwhile, at the Max Cyber Cafe, the de facto file on hostel warden Dr. Chandramani Upadhyay looked something like this:

Name: Dr. Chandramani Upadhyay.

Age: Fifty-five years, seven months, four days.

Marital Status: Married, but left the Mrs. Brahmin back in the village in Uttar Pradesh with six kids. Now lives with his mistress, who writes about women's issues.

Property: Bought two flats and three plots of land in town, but stays in the apartment reserved for the hostel warden. Besides his salary and retirement benefits, he holds several other private insurance policies. Has credit card. He gambles and plays the stock market.

Comment: A classic schemer. A loyal lacquered lackey of Vice-Chancellor Mr. Ashok Agnihotri.

Following this, some student added additional commentary.

Special Edition: Upadhyay-ji pays for all his food with money taken from the hostel fund. He siphons off everything he needs from the bank account of the hostel, buying everything, from his fruits and vegetables to paper and pens to paying for his taxi fare. He's gotten jobs at the university for a couple of nieces and nephews. Upadhyay made some dirt-poor untouchable Dalit student ghostwrite the thesis for his live-in lover, and with it got her conferred a PhD. He's a regularly attending supplicant and darbari at the court held by L. K. Joshi, state minister of the Public Works Department. He claims he's a Marxist but in actuality he's a die-hard Brahminist.

NINE

It was a clear morning, not a cloud in the sky. The sun had finally emerged, radiant and clear. Orange rays of sunshine slanted through a corner of the windowpane of Room 252 and hopped around Rahul's bed like sparrows. O.P. had gone to the bathroom for a shower, and Rahul was gazing out the window as he brushed his teeth next to Madhuri Dixit. Two glasses of chai sat brewing atop a heater in the corner. Chai was served only once a day at the dining hall, with breakfast. But since O.P. and Rahul were both accustomed to gulping down dozens of cups per day, they'd made their own arrangements.

The hostel lay in the hills. The valley sloped down below and ended in a large, level field. On one side were the city hospital, bank, and post office. A residential development was also located in the same area. People played cricket and football on that field. If there had been a telescope in Room 252, you could have seen the whole game without even going there. It was like the university's all-purpose sports field. The road surrounded the field like a semicircle.

Just then, Rahul saw a spot of yellow far away by the residential area slowly making its way along the road. The yellow glowed beautifully in the morning light.

There was something different about this particular yellow. This one entered through his eyes, dissolved in his blood, and went straight to his heart. Rahul felt a quick jump in his heart rate as the thump-thump throbbing reached all the way to his ears.

An odd, intense longing took hold of Rahul, and his room suddenly struck him as tiny and cramped. Where could he get a better, clearer look at that slow-moving spot of yellow? In a few moments it would be hidden behind the photo of Madhuri Dixit's slingshot-wounded backside taped on the window. And then he wouldn't be able to see it. If only he had a pair of binoculars!

There was no doubt: it was the yellow parasol, fluttering gently like the dainty wings of a butterfly, coming toward campus.

It must be her underneath, the one I saw that day. But what if it is really her under that parasol? It was as if Rahul's entire body had been seized by a sweet fever. His heart began to beat faster with a restlessness his body couldn't contain. He held his breath. He eyes remained wide open. A few moments passed like this until, in a blink of an eye, Madhuri Dixit eclipsed the yellow parasol. Shit! Shit! It was unbearable. For the first time ever Rahul felt uncontrollable anger toward Madhuri Dixit and her pretty back. This isn't some film, this is real life, madam. It's not merely an image. This is reality. Understand?

Rahul quickly threw on a pair of pants and a T-shirt. His mouth was still full of toothpaste as he bounded down the stairs, three steps at a time.

He had to reach the bend in the road as quickly as possible, to the place where he could erase all doubt. O god! Let it be her who is carrying that parasol. Let it be her. But what if it's someone else? O god! Whoever is underneath that parasol, just please make it be her! I will be grateful forever.

The shortcut was strewn with rocks and littered with thorny shrubs. Rahul nearly slipped and fell in a few places on loose rocks; after that, he became stealthy like a leopard, without leaving any tracks, and finally arrived at the edge of the lookout point, from where he could hide behind the rocks and watch the road.

Oh! It *was* her, Anjali Joshi, wearing a burgundy sleeveless handloom kurta with light red embroidery. A deep-eggplant-colored chunni was draped over her shoulders. And for sure it was natural vegetable dye, made from flowers and leaves. Wow, so you're an environmentalist, and your taste is ethnic. Wonderful! Where did you buy it? Jaipur? You are simply, simply great. God has made you just so and sent you down here. But you won't be permitted to live in peace in this world. Listen to me. *Come with me—we'll leave the world behind.*

Rahul kicked a rock by accident, which went tumbling down toward the road where Anjali Joshi was walking. It startled her. O god! Those wide, innocent eyes scanned everywhere around before she dared amble forth again. She glanced at the spot where Rahul was hidden, but she turned away, unconcerned. It was as if a startled doe stood watch for a few seconds, only to once again assume its carefree ways.

Rahul's mouth was still filled with toothpaste, which had begun to dissolve and give his breath a sweet minty fragrance. He continued to gaze at her back until after it turned the next bend, passed two neem trees and a wild ber bush, until it finally disappeared behind a big dumb rock. Shit!

He returned to his room to find himself face-to-face with a livid O.P. The two cups of chai brewing on the heater had burned black, filling the room with smoke. "Sorry, yaar . . . very sorry . . . really, I'm sorry . . ."

"Where were you? Look at the dirt and mud on your pants. And you forgot to rinse your mouth out after brushing your teeth?" O.P. glared.

"That's what I'm going to do now, yaar. There was something urgent I suddenly remembered," Rahul said. Then he whispered, "Something to do with the color yellow."

But O.P. didn't hear.

TEN

Rahul was sitting with Gopal Dwivedi in the living room of 18A in the professor's quarters. This living room belonged to the head of the Hindi department, S. N. Mishra: Shri Shyam Narayan Mishra, MA, PhD., DLitt, Crowning Jewel of Literature, etc. Rahul had just come from the Max Cyber Cafe where he had read Mishra-ji's de facto file: *He has two living rooms. One for his sycophant students and unwanted visitors, and a second for his dignitaries and girls.*

So the old Vedic goat indulges in some of the finer things in life, eh?

After a long wait, the curtains rustled, parted, and out came a roundish, potbellied man, the religious tilak mark on forehead, of either Nigerian or Dravidian origin, wearing a homespun lungi around his waist and white undershirt on top. Gopal Dwivedi, who was doing advanced studies in Hindi and, according to the de facto Mishra file, was Mishra's number one student, suddenly lay face down on the carpet and stretched out prostrate, flat as a board. So, this was the chief disciple! Rahul began to panic. What should I do? Which posture should I take? Suddenly he remembered something from *The Mahabharata* or *Om Namah Shiva* or some other series on TV and was saved from some term of address like "good sir!" or "beloved child!" tumbling from his mouth.

"Most Esteemed Honorable Acharya-ji!" is what actually came out.

O.P., Kartikeya, and Pratap Parihar had briefed Gopal Dwivedi extensively and sent him to accompany Rahul. He took to his task with relish. "This is Rahul, sir. He is in the anthropology department in his first year. But he has a deep interest in literature and would like to transfer to the Hindi department."

"But it's already so late. The first semester's nearly finished," Mishra-ji said, eyeing Rahul with total disinterest.

"This student is extraordinarily courteous, disciplined, and obedient, sir. Before this he completed an MSc in organic chemistry," Gopal Dwivedi said in a moment of humility.

"Which division did you score?" Mishra asked, sizing up Rahul for the first time.

"First, sir!" Rahul said. ""Same in graduation."

Rahul clearly saw the smile wiped clean from Mishra's face, replaced by an expression signifying the arrival of indigestion. Gopal Dwivedi at once sensed the change and tried to rescue the moment. "I consider him my younger brother, sir, and as such he shall always require your good grace. He will give his last breath to carry out any command you may give. Take this as my oath—sir!"

The squat frame of that blubbery, buffalo-like creature showed signs of delight for the first time. Under the flared nostrils of his pug nose, a sad excuse for a chuckle emerged from his fixed, fat lips, while his stomach, the size of a Laotian jar, rippled as if it'd been tickled.

Gopal Dwivedi seized the moment and placed a largish clay

pot sealed in a plastic bag on a table beside the acharya: "I went to town at daybreak, and by chance found Vajravasi's shop open. Pandit Jagannath-ji himself called me inside, and absolutely insisted I take this," Gopal Dwivedi said.

"Shakun! Shakuntalaaaaaa! Have some chai sent for these boys!" Raga Jaijaivanti emerged from the acharya's lungs, but with no attention to the melody. For the first time, Rahul felt like things might go his way. Gopal Dwivedi had informed him that if the acharya served them tea, they were as good as gold.

"Our department is full of politics," the acharya announced. "Tell him that his energies should be focused entirely on his research. If he encounters any difficulties, he should liaise straightaway with me or Gopal. No need to involve anyone else. And about tomorrow morning: he should bring his application forms here to me at ten o'clock sharp. By the way, what kind of shape is your thesis in?"

"Only a couple of chapters left, sir. I should have it done by the end of the month. If it weren't for my sister's wedding, I'd be done by now!"

"Yes, of course, I understand. But you should speed things up. I'm feeling pressure to post the results. As long as I'm still around, things can still happen. After me, it's Radha Raman's turn. A real Kanyakubj Brahmin, that one. Pandit Suryakant Tripathi-ji says Raman bites the hand that feeds him. A total ingrate. Meanwhile, every day he's plotting against me with the vice-chancellor. Even our dear Agnihotri-ji is encouraging these elements," the acharya-ji said maliciously.

Then for the first time he softened toward Rahul. "You have an interest in literature. Outstanding. Tell me, what have you read so far? Poetry or prose?"

"A little bit of both, sir-ji!" Who knows why Rahul had the burning desire to add the honorific "ji" after "sir."

"I see. And the names of some writers? Their works?"

"Sir, Dostoyevsky's *Crime and Punishment*, Tolstoy's *War and Peace* and *Resurrection* and short stories. *Old Man and the Sea* and Tagore's *Gora, Gitanjali, The Home and the World*, Garcia Márquez's *Love in the Time of Cholera*, Milan Kundera's *The Joke*, Italo Calvino's *Adam and Eve*, Arundhati Roy's *God of Small . . .*"

"So! Even supermodels are writing modern novels these days, eh? I haven't read anything by her but I've seen that Arundhati on TV in her ad for Lux soap. No doubt. She was Miss World, no? And who wrote that *Old Man?* It rings a bell," the acharya queried.

"Hemingway did, sir! Ernest Hemingway. And sir . . ." Rahul wanted to go on but the acharya cut him short.

"In addition to Western literature, have you read anything Indian?"

"Yes, sir! I've read Premchand's novels, Nirmal Verma's *The Last Wilderness*, Alka Saraogi's *Kali-Katha: Via Bypass*, and Vinod Kumar Shukla's *The Servant's . . .*"

"What about early Hindi verse? Ghananand, Matiram, Bihari, Dev?" the acharya asked.

"No, sir!"

"No Alam, no Bodha?"

"No, sir."

" . . . and Vidyapati and Surdas and Tulsidas . . . ?"

"I've heard of Tulsidas-ji, sir. I saw Ramanand's *Ramayana* TV series, and where I'm from they put on a really great Ram Lila every year around Dusshera. And my mom knows the Sundarkand part by heart."

"Outstanding. Come tomorrow. But if you want to study Hindi deeply then go to the library today and begin reading Ramchandra Shukla's *A History of Hindi Literature.*"

"Which Shukla-ji, Sir?" Rahul blurted out nervously.

"Ha! You . . . ha!" the acharya laughed. "Gopal will tell you everything you need to know. A very intelligent student, he is."

"Yes, sir!"

After finishing their chai, Rahul and Gopal Dwivedi left and took the road back. Dusk had fallen. Shadows faded. Darkness slowly descended.

"Thank you, Gopal-ji. Thank you so much," Rahul said.

Gopal teased him. "An empty 'thank you' isn't going cut it, Rahul-ji. After you get admitted, you'll have to buy a big box of sweets to celebrate."

"Certainly! Certainly! Have faith in me, Dwivedi-ji." Rahul was very happy.

But then Gopal added, "I'm only worried about one little thing. Do you think he—might there have been any confusion about you?"

"What do you mean?" Rahul didn't understand.

"Nothing. I'll take care of it. What I meant was confusion about caste," Gopal said lightly.

Rahul looked toward the sky. The clouds that gather in the evening pour out their rain late into the night. And it would rain tonight. The face of the acharya Shyam Narayan Mishra flashed around in Rahul's head.

Kinnu Da's voice returned. "For thousands of years, countless castes, ethnicities, and cultures kept coming to this country and living in peace. The Scythians, the Huns, the Mongols, the Kushans. Would you be able to find and differentiate all those different groups today?" Kinnu Da asked.

Then he said something Rahul would never forget. "Take any Indian middle-class family, this thing everyone's talking about these days—one that lives in one of the identical Indian metropolises and lives very comfortably. Choose one that has four generations living under one roof, from grandparent to grandchild. Assemble them and take a Grand Family Photograph, just like they do right before 'The End' of a Bombay film. Then enlarge that photo and do a morphological analysis . . . Ha!" Kinnu Da burst out laughing.

"Do you know what you'll find? That one family photo opens up thousands of years of Indian history and places it right at your feet. 'As is the individual, so is the universe': *yat pinde tat brahmande*. It's entirely probable that all of the descendants and offspring of all ethnicities and castes that once upon a time came to this great land will be represented by one single photograph of a middle-class family. But keep in mind there's a part of our society afflicted with a superiority complex. The Great Indian Puritanical Sectarian Casteist Hedonist Homogeneous Middle Class. In that same family you'll find a white, a black, a light brown, a dark brown, a flat nose, a big lips, a long and thin nose, a round eyes, a fine brow, a yellow face. Ha! Everything's mixed in there. The Aryans, Dravidians, Africans, Mongols, Austric, everything."

Kinnu Da grew serious. "In the history of this country's civilization, there was never any voodooland cut off from the rest of the world like in the Andaman Nicobar islands or in Africa or today in the Americas. Here, countless newcomers kept on coming, and once they came, they stayed. Something like 13 to 87 percent of genetic interaction occurred right here. Do you understand the meaning of 'genetic interaction'? It's a relic from an age when there was no AIDS and no condoms! Ha!"

Rahul finally understood what he'd been talking about. So the head of the Hindi department, S. N. Mishra—that dwarfish, fat, pugnosed, fat-lipped tilak-wearing darky, was the fruit of the seed of a foreign mleccha or other non-Aryan sprayed into the womb of some foremother.

The demon devil used the ancient text of *Manusmriti*, the basis of caste, as his ladder to ascend to the top of the sociocultural power structure in the country, and now that he's there, he sits as the head of the caste system. Bastard son of Ravana. If I ever get a chance I'll prepare his gene map and definitely put in his de facto file.

Rahul regarded Gopal Dwivedi. He was rubbing tobacco and lime in his palm, readying it for a chew.

"Gopal-ji, tell me, between Hema Malini from Tamil Nadu, or Dr. S. N. Mishra from Uttar Pradesh, which one do you think is the Aryan? Could you say?"

Gopal rolled the plug tobacco around his tongue and said, "What kind of a question is that?"

"You think it's probably Mishra-ji, no?" Rahul said. He continued, "What about me? What am I: Dravidian or Aryan?"

Gopal Dwivedi began to laugh. "Tsk, tsk, tsk. Forget about the anthropology, dear boy! And go read Ramchandra Shukla's *A History of Hindi Literature*. Tsk, tsk, tsk."

"Hoo! Hoo! Oooga booga!" Rahul made gorilla sounds.

This sound mixed with the rumbling of the clouds and echoed all the way to campus. There was something in it that made Gopal Dwivedi feel a bit uneasy for the first time.

ELEVEN

The next day Rahul spent the entire day in the Hindi department attending to admission formalities, running to and from all
sorts of offices. During lunch he caught up with Anima, Bhagvat,
Raju, Seema Philip, Rana, and Abha, who were all a bit down.
They couldn't understand the sudden whim of Rahul to study
Hindi literature. Even O.P. put in his two cents. "I still can't work
out this stupidity of yours. What are you thinking? Best think
twice, otherwise you'll regret it later."

Rahul smiled and gave O.P. a little pinch. "Yaar, you remember that little bird? Well, she's all grown up and has already ravaged my field. Isn't it a little late for regret?"

"You bastard. As soon as you get into the Hindi department
you start pulling out Hindi proverbs. Why, I oughta . . ."

Rahul took mental note that Anima didn't laugh once. He
couldn't understand why this sad girl was so sad today.

And Rahul didn't even see Anjali Joshi once in the department. Maybe she hadn't come to campus that day.

After dinner, Rahul went out for a night stroll with O.P., Kartikeya, Pratap, and Praveen. They ran into Hemant Barua. It was
the fifth of the month. Attacks from the local goondas usually took
place between the eighth and fifteenth. It was decided that the
SMTF meeting would be at Praveen's the following night, and

that next time they'd take the fight to the goondas themselves. The postman had been seen on campus two days ago. The middle-aged man was bald and decrepit, but shrewd and cunning. The son of a bitch gave the goondas a list of which students got how much in their money orders. No one knew whether he did it because he was afraid of the goondas, or whether he was greedy to get his commission. Rahul had once read a poem in Hindi and seen a Chinese film, both about postmen. But this local letter carrier had made a mockery of those noble characters. The era has descended on humankind where the sole purpose of everyone's life has become money. The Angry Young Hero of prior decades' film fame had transformed in the blink of an eye into the Middle-Aged Greedy Cunning Stock Market Player, and then was appointed game-show host of the superhit of the day, *Who Wants to Be a Millionaire?*

Sapam Tomba's name also came up. He no longer laughed or, for that matter, even spoke much anymore. He'd stopped coming to the badminton court. Considering what he had gone through, everyone could guess why.

Kartikeya and Pratap prevailed upon Madhusudan not to return to Kerala. It was decided that a few students would write a letter to his father and explain that there was no need for him to return. His future wasn't ruined. There was absolutely no need for alarm. Everyone was standing beside him.

So this is what the process of globalization looks like? The whole world will become a village? Everything will turn into America. But if this is really the case, then why does Dr. Watson want to get out of here as fast as possible? Why does Sapam Tomba stand mute? Why is Madhusudan's father telling him to come home? Why was the Christian minister Staines burned alive in his car along with his little children? Why are non-Bengalis afraid in Calcutta and non-Marathis afraid in Mumbai? Why have the few Hindus of Kashmir had to leave their house and land to become refugees, lost, wandering from door to door?

And should only local students from the town be allowed to study here at the university? Locals only as faculty and administrators? It occurred to Rahul that the university and its hostels were like a diorama of the national makeup, now beginning to splinter. Regionalism, casteism, and the muck of cheap petty powers were suddenly seeping out, laying waste to all the great metaphors and federal myths this country had so far constructed.

Rahul had seen a horror movie called *Critters*. Small, round, ugly critters rolling around like balls, gnashing their teeth and eating everything in sight as fast as they could. They'd suddenly appear out of nowhere, a gang of them together, and munch on or destroy whatever lay in their path.

They weren't from here. They were sent to earth from some other planet. Or maybe an alien pod fell to earth, cracked open, and gave birth to them? In no time their numbers multiplied, endlessly. One day they'd consume the entire world, leaving a scene of frightening devastation. It was truly a scary film, and scientific too. It was called "science fiction."

"Hey, take a look over there—that's quite a poster up in front of the library," Pratap pointed.

A three-by-two-foot advertisement was stuck on the wall to the left of the main door where the steps end, showing a girl in a black miniskirt in profile, bust forward, rear end thrust backward, palms facing outward in front of her chest, all of which made her look like the letter S. Huge writing in English below the image read:

Shipra International Enterprises Presents:

First Beauty Casting

Sponsored by Femina India

A golden opportunity to become Miss World and Miss Universe

The greatest chance for your career in fashion, modeling, advertising and acting

Date: 10 September

Day: Sunday

Place: University Auditorium

Time: 9:00–11:30 p.m.

TWELVE

The dates were the fifth to the fifteenth of September.

In these ten days so many events happened one after the other that Rahul felt as if in one sitting he were watching a film in fast-forward, created by a magical device.

The sixth of September was a Wednesday. As soon as he got up, even before brushing his teeth and washing his face, and with eyes half closed, his first order of business was to soak his handkerchief in water and moisten Madhuri Dixit's back so much so that the adhesive loosened, and the center spread of *Stardust* pasted on the window of Room 252 fell to the floor.

The wet paper had become transparent. Traces of advertisements for Honda Hero Splendor and Ile deodorant printed on the other side of the page appeared on Madhuri's eyes and back. Gone were the startled, doe-like eyes and sculpted, tormented back wounded by Salman Khan's slingshot.

Rahul wiped the window until it was spotless. Now he could see clearly the playing field in the valley and the semicircular road surrounding it. From here he could also see with great clarity, without binoculars, like a butterfly could, that shining yellow spot slowly swimming in the distance. Its mere appearance would take Rahul's breath away and rushed the blood fast through his veins.

And the sound of his throbbing heartbeat reached all the way to his ears. Thump, whoosh! Thump, whoosh!

The night has a thousand eyes
and the day but one
yet the light of the bright world dies
with the dying sun

The mind has a thousand eyes
and the heart but one
yet the light of a whole life dies
when love is done!

Rahul stooped down and picked up the pieces of wet paper that had borne Madhuri's photo, opened the door of his room, and threw them outside in the trash.

Arrivederci, Mrs. Nene! Bye-bye!

THIRTEEN

That day Rahul went to the department for the first time in the capacity of a first-year MA student in Hindi. His admission had gone through. Loknath Tripathi was teaching. The topic was "the Bhakti period in Hindi literature." *Bhakti dravidi upaji, laye Ramanand*: "The saint-poets were nourished by the South, and brought by Ramanada." Kabir, Tulsidas, Surdas, Dadu, Mira, Nabhadas, Tukaram, Gyaneshwar.

So, Tripathi-ji, according to you, Surdas and the rest of them were members of Premchand's Progressive Writers' Association in 1936 along with Mulkraj Anand and Sajjad Zahir; and furthermore, that Tulsidas-ji was a Communist Party of India worker who later supported the Emergency, which made Indira Gandhi so happy she awarded him the Padma Vibhushan medal; and if Kabirdas were alive today he'd be having his photo taken accepting a 250,000 rupee award along with the ceremonial coconut and shawl from a company that makes toilets. And, Tripathi-ji, is the extent of your scholarly inquiry to focus exclusively on which Daryaganj book publisher brought out Tulsidas's *Ramcharitmanas* version of the *Ramayana*, and which government minister presided over the launch party? And if Mirabai were with us today, she'd have a post at which institute?

There were a total of eighteen students in the first-year MA

Hindi class: twelve boys and six girls. All of the girls sat next to each other on seats nestled together on the right side of the classroom, as if they were a separate constituency. Chandra, Latta, Sharmishtha, Parvati Mehendale, Shubha Mishra, and her.

Her: in other words, Anjali Joshi.

The creator must have been in a state of deep boredom, fatigue, and uncertainty when he created the young women of the Hindi department. He must have wanted to breathe life into another kind of sentient being: an antelope, giraffe, hippo, crocodile, frog, tortoise, or horse; but in the end, growing tired, he settled on crafting these girls. These sad, weird, dull creatures were created to prove there were exceptions to all norms of proportion of the human figure. Each of the girls brought their own packed lunches from home, and during the break in between periods sat in a group secluded from the others and ate, chatting away. One day the girls decided they had to do their PhDs together as a group, and the next day they decided anew that each should be married off. Despite it all, they chirped away like birds, and when they laughed, their eyes shone brilliantly, they smiled revealing their teeth, so they'd try to cover their faces with the edge of their saris or dupattas. To watch them was like being in the era of films such as *Uran Khatola, Anmol Ghari, Bhavare Nain,* and *Barsaat.* The most modern girl of the group had bought some cheap readymade jeans from a roadside stall and wore them with a mismatched top or T-shirt that gave her the look of an extra from a Tamil film or, if one felt kind, like Sadhana, the heroine of the film *Mera Saya,* whose painstakingly coiffed bouffant concealed an upside-down stainless steel cup to give it the right shape. And the male students were cut from the same cloth. In the Hindi department Rahul felt he'd been transported by time machine to another place and time.

And in the middle of the group was Anjali Joshi.

Was she Alice temporarily passing through Wonderland? Or did her magical body house that sort of soul chemically processed from desi ghee, mango pickle, pious fasting, devotional singing, proper seasoning, home economics, Bombay cinema, and romance novels?

But it was recorded in the diary for the sixth of September that Rahul's fears were baseless. At three o'clock all his old friends showed up. Anima, Rana, Abha, Raju, Neera Didi, and Renu. All went to the canteen. Anjali Joshi was also with them. On their way, they had the good fortune not to run into any local goondas who might have taunted them.

A cup of chai and samosas all around: this was the celebration of Rahul's admission to the Hindi department. He'd just gotten paid from his tutoring job, so the days of being broke were still a ways off.

"You'll rot in there, Rahul," Rana said. "When did you get possessed with this idea of studying Hindi literature? It's still a complete mystery to us."

"What are you going to do with this degree? Get a lousy academic job? You should study something that's in demand. Some of the students in that department can't do anything else. And others were brought in by tradition. Do you know? Dr. Tripathi, Awasthi, Mishra, Tiwari-ji—every year they try as hard as they can to keep the department from shutting down," Raju informed everyone.

"That Balram Pandey does all the cooking at Tripathi's house," Neera Didi said.

"*I* know why Rahul transferred to the Hindi department," Anima declared, breaking her silence for the first time. She said it in a way that made Rahul feel as if there was something crawling up his spine.

"Why did he do it?" Neera Didi asked.

"Should I tell them?" Anima gave Rahul a piercing stare.

"Go ahead!" Rahul's throat went dry and his face became solemn like an anxious child who wanted to keep a little secret hidden from everyone.

"Should I tell them?" Anima said again in a cold, lifeless, yet firm voice.

"Tell us! Why make a mystery of it?" Neera Didi began to get angry. Everyone's eyes fixed on Anima.

Anima stood and placed her hand on Anjali's shoulder—

"Anjali, can you tell us why Rahul dropped out of the anthropology department and took admission in Hindi?"

"What do you mean?" Anjali's eyes opened wide.

"This is what I mean. If you hadn't gotten jaundice, and hadn't done so badly on your exams, then you would have been admitted to some other department, and you wouldn't have come to our department that day to eat corn, and this poor boy would still be an anthropology student!" Anima said. Everybody laughed.

Anjali Joshi took a good look at Rahul for the first time. Try as Rahul might to laugh it off, there was something in his voice that made him sound guilty as charged.

FOURTEEN

It was something like a light fever, or a mild buzz, that began to consume Rahul on Wednesday, the sixth of September, at three thirty-five p.m. He couldn't utter a word. It was such a deep and dizzying silence it seemed as if his very sense of being was lost inside it. It was a totally new and unique experience, the first like it in his life.

He came in and lay down on his bed in Room 252 even before the sun had set. Just that morning he had scrubbed the windowpane clear with his handkerchief. He got up a few times to look out the window. The green and brown vegetation and trees in the valley stood quietly in the evening light. The normally dull rock outcroppings scattered here and there now shone with a golden hue. On the broad, flat field, the shadows of the trees elongated with every passing moment.

Rahul's eyes scanned the distance for any sign of that spot of yellow, which just might be returning to the residential development. Anjali's face flashed through his mind again and again like a bolt of lightning. In his mind she was even now on her way to see him. He held his eyes shut and froze her image in his imagination.

There was no anger in those eyes, but rather the ache from being stung by the slingshot pellet, and her eagerness.

When did Rahul finally doze off? He wasn't sure. O.P. shook

him awake. "No dinner? It's been dinnertime for awhile. You're not sick, are you?"

Stumbling, Rahul managed to pull himself out of bed. He stumbled to the bathroom, turned on the tap, and put his head under the rush of water. It was as if the water were an entirely new sensation, cool and fresh. He'd fallen asleep sometime around six o'clock and now it was eight thirty. A long period of time had elapsed during this two-and-a-half-hour nap. Everything before had been part of a former existence; this was like a new life entirely, a feeling of a light fever and intoxication.

Rahul splashed cold water on his eyes. I'm slowly waking up, aren't I?

"I'll meet you down in the dining hall, I'm heading out," O.P.'s voice sounded from outside.

Rahul later bumped into Hemant Barua in the dining hall, who sometimes stopped by after beating Professor Aggrawal in a game of chess. Hemant had two items of news. One was that he hadn't seen Sapam Tomba, whose door was locked, for two days.

The second was the announcement that Rahul had made a terrifying mistake in taking admission to the Hindi department because every last individual in the department, from the sweeper to the chair, was a Brahmin. Save for Rahul, Shaligaram, and Shailendra George, the rest of the first-year Hindi students were all Brahmins.

Hemant Barua, the wondrous number-crunching genius from Dibrugarh, Assam, and MSc in the Department of Mathematics, combined statistics, information, and facts into a single process. He declared that on the basis of caste, the Brahmin to non-Brahmin ratio was approximately 88 percent to 12 percent. What's more, those who left with their PhDs and later found work reflected the same statistic. Barua said, "Rahul, you have entered a labyrinth where they will lynch you one day. Beware. It's not too late."

Both pieces of information worried Rahul. Where had Sapam gone? The image of the handsome, roly-poly boy from Imphal flashed before his eyes.

The night passed, somehow, though Rahul was not conscious.

But in that state of unconsciousness a yellow parasol quietly fluttered like a butterfly coming up the hills from the valley below on the semicircular road, and each moment stretched out for such an eternity that his sleep was encircled from below him. Rahul, deep inside, slept without a care in the world, like an innocent, orphaned baby.

It was something like after the apocalypse that ends creation, when a tiny god resting on a tiny leaf rides the waves of a fathomless sea, asleep, engrossed in the redreaming of his next creation.

FIFTEEN

Some sort of predetermined rule dictated that Rahul's first, and best, friends would be Shailendra George and Shaligaram. The three of them, instinctively, of their own accord, began to sit together. They talked among themselves and discovered that each of the other students had some sort of connection, either with one another, or with the teachers, or some family connection, or they had some other basis for rapport. These were confident boys who didn't have to worry about their future. They were chiefly foot soldiers in the political machinations of the department. Less interested in books and literature, they took greater interest in the tricks of the trade that would help get their hands on degrees, positions, promotions, and fellowships. And they were very quick to master their training. There was some gene in their DNA that allowed them to learn this knowledge with the same ease a squirrel learns to scramble up a tree or a fish how to swim in the water or a kingfisher how to dive or a bandicoot how to make a hole in a wall and sneak in the house.

Shailendra George said that when his family had still been Hindu, his father had been an untouchable in charge of the cremation grounds. He'd converted from Hinduism thirty years ago.

Shaligaram was a weaver by caste. He said that upper-caste people, particularly Brahmins, made up jokes and sayings as proof of the idiotic ways weavers act. One joke goes that once upon a time a weaver had a dream that five two-hundred-pound jute sacks, normally filled with grain, were lying behind the house stuffed with rupees next to a pile of firewood. The weaver awoke and, remembering his dream, immediately marched out back. When he arrived, you can't imagine his surprise when he found five sacks, as real as can be, lying next to the pile of wood. He shouted for all his neighbors to come, and once they were gathered, he told them all about the dream.

The weaver's neighbors saw that millions of rupee notes and coins stuffed the five sacks. First they conferred among themselves. They then turned to the weaver to explain that, yes, the gunnysacks indeed contained a great harvest of wealth. But there was a lot of chaff and only a bit of grain. So they instructed him to separate and get rid of the worthless chaff and keep only the valuable grain.

The joke continues that the weaver's womenfolk sifted out the chaff: the paper bills in denominations of 500, 100, 10, and 20, which, like chaff, is carried off by the wind. The weaver's womenfolk kept only the grain. With five full bags, they managed to collect the quarter-, half-rupee coins, pennies, and cowries totaling something like 2,500 rupees.

Divvying up the spoils, the neighbors all became millionaires, while the dreaming weaver became a "pennyaire" and hero of this caste joke. It's interesting that countless such jokes have gone around about lower-caste people; the punch line is always followed by the sound of a belly laugh, a dark echo that has rung through the centuries.

Goondas have a long tradition of these kinds of jokes about simple, honest castes, communities, or men who get tricked. Each joke ends with the same kind of mass laughter: cruel, dripping, self-satisfied, uncivilized, full of power.

The same sort of group guffaw could be heard in the Hindi department during the break between classes, when Balram Pandey, who served as cook for Dr. Loknath Tripathi, told a new weaver joke. The girls, as a group, had already slipped outside to eat apart from the rest, carrying their little tiffin food cylinders filled with parathas they'd brought from home.

Balram Pandey's weaver joke went like this: Once upon a time a weaver got married. The next day his upper-caste friends from the neighborhood asked him, "So, did you feed your new bride a little snack at night?" The weaver had, in fact, fed his wife all sorts of sweet desserts like laddus, motichurs, and a whole string of jelabis, and said so to his friends.

The weaver's friends started to laugh to themselves that this idiot doesn't know a thing, and this imbecile hasn't even the good sense to feed a snack to his new bride's other mouth. The poor girl must still be hungry. And he doesn't even realize that women's other mouth must be fed with something else entirely, not just with jelabis and motichur.

The weaver pleaded with his friends to tell him what kind of sweet dessert he should feed his new bride. His friends felt sorry for the weaver's ignorance and gave him some advice: first take a toothbrush and toothpaste, clean and rinse out your bride's other mouth, and then give us a call. We'll come and bring her the snack ourselves. After all, what are friends for?

The joke continues that meanwhile the weaver went to ask his new bride about her other mouth and other stomach. Even though the wife was simple and uneducated like the weaver, she put two and two together and, blushing, showed her second mouth to her new husband. He proceeded to use the toothbrush and toothpaste given by his friends to thoroughly clean his wife's other mouth. Then he let them know he'd done as he was told.

His friends came over and, one after another, they took turns serving breakfast, lunch, and dinner to the weaver's new bride.

The joke produced a great outburst of laughter among the first-year MA Hindi students in class. A fiery, seething, base, inhuman laugh that had prevailed for centuries.

Rahul looked at Shailendra George and Shaligaram. Of the twelve students, the three of them sat off to one side, the other nine to the other. The laughing came from that side. Imagine a furnace in a steel plant in Bokaro or Bhilai, with temperatures of thousands of degrees, glowing bright red, liquid pig iron flowing so hot that it would vaporize a man into thin air—this laughter flashed even hotter than that. It wasn't even the sound of laughter; it was the sound of a medieval fire disgorging caste abhorrence like lava from the Vedic furnace poured right into their ears.

Rahul watched all their laughing faces. Vimal Shukla, Vinod Vajpayi, Balram Pandey, Vijay Pachauri, Kamal Tripathi, Ram Narayan Chaturvedi, Sudip Pant, Vibhuti Prasad Mishra. All of them were "critters," like from the movie. Ball-like, rolling, frightening, omnivorous critters sent from another world or demon realm to this bit of earth. Or else they arrived in a mysterious pod dropped from the skies, which then exploded. The creatures emerged on their own and over time established their own system of rule. They were everywhere. In language, in politics, in temples, in Parliament, in civil service, in places of worship, in birth, at death; from food and water to clothing and medicine to all media of information—newspapers, books, universities, TV channels; from finance to poetry, from art to letters.

These were the critters. When they came to this part of the world, the first thing they did was gobble up the sun in order to project a darkness into history, so dark that inside it no one could see the advance of their ever-hungry jaws and glimmering, razor-sharp teeth. They devoured the Buddha, the tales about his life, the sublime philosophies of the Upanishads, and all manner of folktales. They gnawed Jesus, Moses, Pirs, prophets, and Sufi saints down to the bones, crushed the bones into fertilizer, threw the fertilizer into a pit where a poisonous tree took root, and bore fruit—fruit that's been hanging in the psyche of millions of innocent inhabitants of this part of the world for centuries.

Insult and disgust stained Shaligaram's face first the color of mud, then to black. Fear shone from the eyes of Shailendra George.

"Shut up! Hold your filthy tongue! Bastards!" Rahul stood up. "Hindi literature and Hindu dharma have taught you this? Demon sons of Ravana! When will you stop eating? How much of this world will you destroy? You're like weevils, leeches, gnats—parasites sucking on the broken body of this great country. Don't forget that Ravana was one of *you*, living on the golden island of Lanka. It was still the treta-yug, when the dharma bull still had three legs, when you abducted the wife of the exiled Ram from their household, and then tore her up from the inside. It was a senseless life of never-ending wandering! And you bastards pretend to be devotees of Ram? Now in this kali-yug of the twentieth and twenty-first centuries, when the dharma bull has but one leg, you are fashioning Ram into your very own barbaric, violent, murderous, fundamentalist, misanthropic, fascist image! Because you need the votes. Because you have to cling to power. Because now you need more to eat.

"How many thousands of years do you need power? If you want to know the truth, you bastards, here it is. The Huns never really held power in this country. Neither did the Scythians, the Kushans, the Greeks, the Mughals, or the English. Each of these regimes was just a cover for your Raj. The machete blade that's come down for centuries on the neck of every honest, meek man who stands for justice is really just a symbol of your political power. If you have been so ennobled, then tell me: why wasn't god ever born a Brahmin?"

Rahul was shaking with rage. But the dark stain had been wiped from Shaligaram's face, and Shailendra George didn't seem frightened anymore.

Just then, Dr. Loknath Tripathi entered the room. "Is there some kind of meeting going on here? Oh, right, of course, you're all getting ready for the Union Council elections. But which candidate was giving the speech?"

The group of girls also returned. Now the medieval devotional literature lesson would begin, given by Dr. Loknath Tripathi, at whose house Balram Pandey worked as a cook, and who would one day become head of this Hindi department.

The three o'clock class was over. Thick tension suddenly cast its shadow throughout the entire classroom. Rahul felt as if he was suffocating. He stepped outside into the corridor. From there he could see the library. Next to it were two leafy neem trees; the shade beneath them must be deliciously cool.

As Rahul stood there, Kartikeya, O.P., Pratap, and a few others came running over.

"Sapam committed suicide. He's dead." Kartikeya's face trembled. Everyone was out of breath.

"They found his body in the old well behind the hostel."

There was a deep silence, screaming and ringing even in the absence of sound. Like after a falling meteor breaks up, or after a big explosion, or after a horrific death.

Rahul's mind went still. No sound reached his ears. He fell in step behind his friends like a robot.

In the cool shade of the neem tree near the library stood Chaitanya—Chaitanya, the great master. But there was no singing of kirtans; the man was silent. His body was covered with scratches. His brow was disfigured. A bullet may have pierced a hole right between his eyes, sending a steady stream of blood flowing over his eyes.

A broken dholak lay on the ground, with a kartal and tiny set of cymbals next to the drum. And next to them, corpses. The police, Border Security Force, Central Reserve Police Force, a band of terrorists, a gang of Mafiosos, a fundamentalist, the Taliban or Hizbul or the Ranbir Sena, some Naxalites, Acchan Guru, Dawood, and the secret service detail of some government minister—all combined in a joint operation, and, after some wild firing, had shot them dead.

Behind the neem tree stood Gandhi's assassin, Nathuram Godse, smoke coming from his gun.

Chaitanya's mouth was still moving to sing the next line of the devotional kirtan song, but the only sound coming out was a near-silent *bhaanya bhaanya bhaanya.*

Rahul realized that on the grass next to his feet and the broken dholak was Sapam's body.

"I'll kill myself someday, I really will. Mark my words! How can I go on? Tell me? My brother sent me money for my studies. Now I'll fight for my freedom. Do you know what they did to me . . . ?"

White ducks ran everywhere; drops of blood stained their feathers. A wind blew through the dry bamboo grove playing thousands of bamboo trees like the bansuri. They'd learned how to play the flute from Krishna, whom Rukmini came there to meet.

Sapam's brother stared silently at him with his dead eyes. His father played the dholak and sang.

Rahul burst into tears. O.P. and Kartikeya tried to calm him down. "Try to pull yourself together, Rahul!"

Anjali Joshi stood silently in the corridor, watching.

SIXTEEN

It was nine thirty at night. Dinner hadn't been served in the hostel. A unanimous decision was reached by all of the students of Tagore Hostel as part of the mourning for Sapam. Notices were tacked up in front of the dining hall that students wishing to eat could go to B. B. Desai Hostel.

Later it turned out that aside from a few dining hall staff and a stray student, nobody had eaten dinner that night.

It revealed a deep sense of sorrow born from Sapam's suicide. The students spoke very little to one another, and even at that in feeble voices, as if their throats were constricted. Was it merely the sadness over Sapam's sudden death that had weakened their voices so—or was there also a newfound fear inside each student that had disarmed their voices, rendering them weak and powerless? Even the most argumentative and boisterous among them, those who talked the loudest, today were silent. The sounds of motorcycles were menacing. Someone arriving to pick up a friend would sound the horn on his motorcycle instead of calling out for his friend on the top floor of the hostel. No one called out to anyone.

The bulb in the corridor gave off a grimy, gloomy light. In the hazy darkness, the sound of the boys' conversation, halting and subdued, was only occasional, like blurry silhouettes traversing a movie screen.

Rahul, Kartikeya, Pratap, Masood, O.P., and Praveen were walking on the rocky pathway covered with shrubs and undergrowth that led from the area behind B. B. Hostel. The police had been at the scene all day long, and aside from a few university staff, no one had been allowed there. The crowd of students had been kept at a distance from where they couldn't see the place Sapam had committed suicide. Some students wanted to try to climb a tree in order to see better, but there were only bushy acacia. There was a semal tree, but it was full of thorns.

By seven in the evening, the police had completed their investigation of the site and withdrawn. Sapam's body was transferred to the morgue at Gandhi Hospital. The postmortem was scheduled for the next day. His classmates tried everything they could to have a look at Sapam's body, but they were refused. Vice-Chancellor Agnihotri had called to inform the chief secretary of Manipur, it was said. Sapam's father could come from Imphal; otherwise, Sapam's body would be sent there by train. There was no money to have his body flown home.

Rahul wondered how Sapam's father would take the news. It hadn't been long since his oldest son, a primary school teacher in Singjamei, near Imphal, had been shot dead by the police, mistaken for a terrorist. And now all that remained of his youngest son Sapam was a corpse brought to the morgue a few hours ago. He, too, wouldn't last long after this. Would he come here to perform Sapam's last rites? Or he'll get the news and have such a breakdown that he won't be able to make the long three-day trip—from Imphal to Kohima to Guwahati to Delhi via Bongaigaon to Agra to Gwalior to Jhansi to here.

The bitter truth is that Sapam, his father, and hundreds of millions of their unfortunate countrymen are not among those for whom technology has made the world a smaller place, or has eradicated distance. There are others who consider the U.S., France, and Germany just like their own backyards. Whenever the mood strikes, they mosey over to wash their faces and take a piss.

Kartikeya held a flashlight in his hand. They pushed their way through the motley scrub of thick sirkin, lentina, chakvar, and besharam bushes, until finally they arrived at the well into which Sapam had jumped and taken his life.

There was something about the place—as soon as they arrived, some thick thing covered their consciousness like a blanket. It was like a physical numbing, yet something that radiated a kind of shudder throughout all their bodily channels. They all felt as if suddenly Sapam would appear sitting on the broken rocks that formed a skirt around the edge of the well in the middle of all this undergrowth and declare, "Oh, I get it—you guys came here to get me to come to dinner! You go ahead, I'm on my way . . ."

It was a very old well that hadn't been in use for ten years. It must have been bored by hand. The soil here was rocky and craggy. It had to have been painstaking labor to dig this decent sized a well, inch by inch. The locals call it an indaara. Just think of all the iron that was ground down from the hoes, crowbars, and pickaxes used to dig seventy feet deep. It was constructed when there were no drill bores. It was said that this well used to supply the entire university. Now the main water station is located on another hillock.

Kartikeya shined his flashlight into the well. Roots, shrubs, and dry clumps of grass grew from the inside of the well. This growth encircled a darkness extending to the bottom of the wall, where far beneath lay the water. Supposedly, it was a very deep well. The light from the flashlight just reached the water level in the depth of that darkness. They couldn't make out anything clearly, just reddish-green hues twinkling in the beam of yellow light. "How did Sapam find this particular well?" Kartikeya asked in a quiet, uneven voice.

"He said something about this once," Praveen said. "I guess—I guess he'd been thinking about it for quite some time."

"What other choice did he have? The reality is that even before committing suicide he'd already been done in," said Masood.

"He should have become a terrorist. Then he could have taken revenge on everyone—the people who killed his brother, the people who stole his money and tried to sodomize him," said Pratap Parihar.

"That's not the right way to think about this," Kartikeya said, suddenly roused. His voice had become more serious and firm, cold and tough like metal. He switched off the flashlight and said in the darkness, "Even after this horror you still can't grasp the truth of who's the terrorist and who's the criminal?"

After this utterance of Kartikeya Kajle from Pune, the only sounds that could be heard were the night insects and the boys' own breathing, such was the deep silence that spread through the darkness. The stillness, wordless and tense, combined with the tragedy of Sapam, awoke a surge of inner disquietude that made it hard to think straight at all. The calm was hardly peaceful, but rather anxious, disturbed, and suffocating.

Seventy feet below, in the depths of darkness, where the faint yellow light from the flashlight caught the surface of the water in reddish-green sparkle, Rahul sensed something floating. He touched Kartikeya on the shoulder. "I think there's something down there. A bit to the right. Now up a little more."

The dim light hardly reached the depths of the well, but there in its beam Rahul could make out one of Sapam's sandals, floating on the surface. Two months ago, just after he and Rahul had become friends, Sapam had bought a pair of them in town at the Liberty shoe store.

Rahul wished he could somehow climb down deep into the well to retrieve the sandal. What awful irony. This plastic, inanimate, 40-rupee sandal that had come into being in Sapam's life a short two months ago still exists, floating on the surface, while a real life was no more. Vanished in the shimmering water.

Not a word was spoken as they returned to the hostel. It seemed that Sapam himself had emerged from somewhere amid the bushes and shrubs, trailing behind them in the darkness. Head bowed, from the depth of his death. That must have been why Kartikeya shined the flashlight behind a few times. When he did, there was nothing. Only rocks, shrubs, and thorny, dried-out acacia.

As they passed through the corridor of the hostel they saw Room 212, Sapam Tomba's room. The police and university administration had sealed off the room. An unfamiliar heavy-duty lock had been fastened to the door. The lock was frightening to behold. Peering out from behind it was Sapam's death.

Rahul was wide awake late into the night. O.P. was just across the room in his bed against the far wall. He couldn't fall asleep either, but neither spoke. It was a noiselessness neither had the strength to shatter. A few steps down the hall was Sapam's room where he'd been living just four days ago.

At that moment, Sapam's bloated body lay in town at the mortuary of the Mahatma Gandhi Hospital. How must his sweet, round face look now? The mortuary wasn't even air-conditioned; dead bodies were laid out on ice blocks. The word was that the hospital workers pocketed even the money set aside for the ice.

SEVENTEEN

The next day—the seventh of September—was declared a day off. This was the routine and formality the university followed when mourning the death of a student, in this case one named Sapam Tomba, from Manipur, who was in the first year of his MSc.

At ten o'clock, Rahul and Hemant Barua decided for no particular reason to leave the hostel and take a walk toward campus. It was dead quiet and the department buildings were closed. Dogs and crows hovered in front of the canteen. The entire area felt uninhabited.

"Sapam used to say that the young generation of Manipuris were quickly dropping the Hindu last names once affixed to the end of their own," Hemant said. "They want to get back to their tribal roots. We're ashamed at the idiocy of our forefathers, who were made the fools for so long. The same winds of change are blowing in Assam, too. We have to ask ourselves, 'Are we really Indian?'"

"Who is really Indian then?" Rahul asked. "The professional politicians, con men, criminals, corrupt bureaucrats, middlemen, and businessmen who live in Delhi, U.P., and Bihar—are they the only Indians?" Rahul was getting wound up. "They've hijacked our independence. Since India's not a proper nation-state, how can anyone say they're Indian?"

"But don't forget, my dear, about Indian nationalism. Didn't you see it happening just now during the Kargil War—what else do you think it was! Our boys coming from our very own Guwahati, Silchar, and Dibrugarh gave their lives up there, don't you know."

Rahul began to laugh, and Hemant Barua followed suit.

"Sponsored nationalism! Now explain this to me, Hemant, have you ever heard of a kind of nationalism that exists only in terms of another country?" Rahul asked.

"What do you mean?" Hemant asked.

"What I mean is, why is it that whenever the flag of nationalism is raised, it's always in terms of Pakistan? Why don't feelings of nationalism get stirred up when faced with a certain other very powerful country? One that made us slaves and sent fleets of ships full of arms in order to destroy our country—and those arms, once here, killed countless people. When it comes to them, we just wag our tails like a good little lapdog." Rahul was now animated.

Rahul wondered if it's true that all former frames of reference are now immaterial, and if it's true we've reached the end of history? Have the memories of this nation's rulers and ruled been destroyed? Or maybe these times are simply ones of total change. This is a new world, a new world order where the entire terrain of the past is irrelevant. If this is true, how come so much "nationalism" of the past is stirred up when atomic bombs explode in Pokharan, or as a reaction to the Kargil War, or to violence in Kashmir? Is this nationalism the real thing, or just some brand of foul hate among religious communities—a hate intentionally awakened? Given the entire historical context, think of how utterly changed our relationship is now with England and America. So why are ancient matters from Babar and Aurangzeb's time continually stirred up? If the Mughal emperor Babar's mosque, the Babri Masjid, should never have been built in Ayodhya, as some Hindu extremists allege it was constructed over the birthplace of Ram, why isn't it considered just as wrong to have built Lutyens's Viceroy House, where the president of this country lives? And why isn't India Gate just as wrong, the place where just a few years ago, fifty years of India's independence was celebrated with great pomp and circumstance, and where A. R. Rahman sang "Ma, Tujhe Salaam"? If those British-built structures haven't been torn down, then why that one in Ayodhya?

Rahul's thoughts were taking him to a strange place. It was that night, the fifteenth of August, 1997, and as the TV broadcast songs sung in celebration of the Golden Jubilee of independent India, Rahul watched and listened, shivering with excitement, his eyes brimming with tears for his country, when, all of a sudden, he began to experience the moment in a different sort of way. He'd heard that the song sung in the temple in Bankimchandra's Bengali novel *Anandamath* by the holy ascetics who lived there was sung against the "Yavanas," or Muslim rulers at the time. The name of the song was "Vande Mataram," by Bhavananda. This song is considered practically the second national anthem of India. At the time, to sing this song signified opposition to British rule and was considered seditious. Maybe this had been Bankimchandra's intention all along. The holy ascetics of *Anandamath* who sang this song wore the typical saffron-colored robes.

Rahul instantly remembered the photographs in newspapers and magazines of the people who'd climbed atop the dome of the

Babri Masjid in 1992. The people sitting atop that dome wore the same saffron-colored clothes. So was it Bhavananda and the same holy ascetics who climbed out of Bankimchandra's novel and, on December 6, 1992, climbed up the dome and tore it down? And was it the same group who in 1997 had that song translated into Hindustani and had it sung by A. R. Rahman in Delhi, at India Gate, on the occasion of the Golden Jubilee of India's independence? But those people were characters in a novel created by Bankimchandra in opposition to British rule! So why were these people singing that song—in what seemed to be a demonstration that they are the new rulers of India—standing beneath a Lutyens-built monument dating from the colonial era? Hidden inside the "nationalism" expressed by the song was hatred of Babar's mosque from the Mughal Raj and slavery to Lutyens's buildings from the British Raj. So they weren't the revolutionary religious ascetics from Bankimchandra's *Anandamath* at all, but others in disguise, whose nationalism was founded on the principles of malice toward Muslims and kissing English ass. And isn't that why this brand of nationalism takes up arms exclusively against Pakistan, but when confronted with the new colonial powers of the West, lifts its tail and begins wagging it? *Atta boy! Good doggie!*

"Hemant, do you know what Lutyens, the man the great Indian middle-class elite are so proud of and the man who built the Viceroy House in Delhi and all sorts of other buildings of time, used to say about Indians?"

"No, what?" Hemant asked eagerly.

"He used to say that the dirtiest, ugliest, most barbarous race in the world were the natives of India. He subscribed to the theory that Indians were Darwin's 'missing link' between apes and humans. To him they were semi or half human or, at most, a 'developed' orangutan," Rahul said.

"Really? Where did you read that?" Hemant asked.

"Pick up a copy of William Dalrymple's *City of Djinns.* Dalrymple wrote that one evening as the sun was going down he stood at India Gate and looked at Rashtrapati Bhavan, the Luytens-built Viceroy House, and while looking at the building with the sun setting behind, a chill went up his spine. The architectural style of this building reminded him of two others, images of which flashed through his mind. The first was of architecture in Milan during the time of Mussolini, and the second was of Hitler's Berlin. All three styles shared the same bewildering majesty, meant to keep man under control, with a style of architectural menacing as if cursed. Dalrymple wrote that the British Empire, Nazi Germany, and Italian Fascism all maintained a balance between secrecy and intimidation." Rahul's voice trembled as if it were coming from inside a deep well. In that well, on the water's surface, floated Sapam's sandal after his suicide.

"It's frightening to think that the number one citizen of this country, guardian of our constitution and commander of the three branches of our armed forces, lives in that building."

So said Rahul, hardly twenty-three years old, who, in his dizzying infatuation for Anjali Joshi, dropped out of the anthropology department only to become a first-year student in the Hindi department.

"Rahul, I have calculated a list of data about Assam. If the rulers in Delhi were to leave Assam, and the people of Assam were to take control of their own natural resources, do you know what would happen? Assam's per capita income would be greater than that of the United Arab Emirates. Assam would be the richest country in the world, but now it's among the poorest and most backward in India. And the same applies to nearly every other state."

So said Hemant Barua, himself hardly twenty-one, who had come here to do an MSc in mathematics at the same time he was enrolled in an e-commerce course at a private IT school.

Rahul wondered which "new generation" in India would be the one to shape the days to come. Would it be the new "X-Y" generation seen on TV, in movies, fashion shows, and in colorful English-language newspapers published in Bombay-Delhi-Calcutta-Bangalore, drinking Pepsi, playing cricket, dancing to pop music like hippies with half-naked girls? Or would it be the generation of those running off to America, Canada, and Germany, spitting on all of their parents' values and beliefs and giving them a kick on the way out the door, just to make as much money as possible in a job with a big multinational corporation?

Or would it be the generation of those living in the dirt-poor, hellish places of Assam, Mizoram, Manipur, Andhra, Kashmir, Bihar, and Tamil Nadu, arming themselves with AK-47s and home-made explosives, taking part in desperate acts of sabotage and violence? Or would it be the generation of those taking their lives every day out of despair from lack of daily bread? Which is the new generation? The one with a Pepsi in hand, half-naked model on his arm, Visa card in the pocket; or him, the one with red eyes, whose parents have been plundered for fifty years by successive regimes, who has a weapon in hand and is killed every day in "encounters"?

Who was this freedom created for, the freedom that the old saint of Sabarmati gave birth to some fifty years ago, with neither shield nor sword but with only his own charisma, singing, *Vaishnav jan to tene kaheye je pir paraai jaane re?* Is that why they shot him dead, so he couldn't perform his wonders in the future?

Rahul and Hemant regarded one another with blank expressions. The campus was deserted; an empty wasteland in which even the trees stood as lifeless as statues, sunk in mourning.

> Not a moment of peace, my friend
> Not a moment of rest, my friend
> And no end in sight

Both of them started singing the song together, quietly. It was a pop song, very popular these days among students on campus, a song sung by Brian O'Connell, Salman Ahmed, and Ali Azmat of the band Junoon in memory of Nusrat Fateh Ali Khan.

It was surprising that this recording was of Pakistani pop singers. Could it be that an identical feeling of disquiet that transcended political boundaries and grew stronger every day had seized the hearts of all the simple, everyday people living throughout the whole subcontinent? It's a bit like when fire spreads through the cramped part of town, showing no concern for whose house is burning, or whose fence, or whose gate, or whose name is inscribed on the nameplate hanging outside the door. A natural, innate, genuine fire. Agni, the same Agni that performs and concludes all sacrifices of fire.

Indram jagat sarvam daheyam bhasmikuryam yad endam sthivaradi prithivyam! Agni: the god of fire that reduces to ashes all that is visible in this world!

Not a moment of peace, my friend
Not a moment of rest, my friend
And no end in sight

Rahul felt as if someone with vast unseen hands was quietly writing a grand new national anthem on the beating hearts of the more than 1 billion simple, honest, robbed, cheated, oppressed, and tormented residents of this enormous South Asian subcontinent, a completely new song that, one day, would be sung in unison by the voices of tens of millions, echoing over the whole land. A New Mega National Song!

Would there again be a widespread mutiny, this time against the Western corporate Raj, throughout all of South Asia? This time too, like in 1857, would the struggle for independence be brutally crushed by the army of the "Indian corporate government" and, afterward, would a half-naked, loincloth-wearing man emerge out of this darkness as the new symbol for the wretched and cheated, to challenge—unarmed—the corrupt Brahmin-businessman market system of the financiers, criminals, and thugs? This Market Empire on which again the sun never sets he would set for them once more, either in the Bay of Bengal or in the Indian Ocean.

Or would another Nathuram point-blank make the saint sleep the sleep of death? And then seize power?

Hé Ram!

Hemant put an arm around Rahul's shoulder and whispered, "See, see, look over there!"

Rahul looked. Under the shade of the neem tree next to the

library, where yesterday stood Chaitanya, now lay the yellow parasol. It was the same yellow color that entered his eyes, floated through his veins, and swam in his blood. Music warmed by a sweet, lapping flame within began to hum inside Rahul. His blood carried the music of his heartbeat ringing clearly in his ears.

Dhak . . . dhak . . . dhak . . .

Next to the parasol in the shade of the neem tree was Anima and her, Anjali Joshi. Rahul stood, mute. Hemant took his hand. "She's all yours. C'mon, let's go over there and talk with them."

"I'd rather not," Rahul said, reluctant, but Hemant had already taken hold of his hand and was leading him in their direction.

Anima and Anjali were happy to see Hemant and Rahul. They'd come in the hope that the library might be open, but it was closed, so the two had plunked themselves down right there.

"The student who passed away—he was your friend?" Anjali asked Rahul. Yesterday she'd been watching as Rahul cried in the corridor of the department.

"Sapam was a wonderful kid. He lived in our hostel, on my floor," Rahul said. "We played badminton together."

"Haven't the police arrested the goondas who attacked and robbed him?" Anjali asked, concerned.

"What can the police do? Where's the evidence against them?" Rahul said.

"The same police shot his big brother dead in Imphal," Hemant said angrily. "Every day organized criminals kill innocent people. The media hides this daily news."

"You should speak with your father! He's a state minister, he might be able to do something," Anima said, turning to Anjali.

"What's the point of that? It's only because of the goondas that he's a state minister." Startled, Anjali looked at Rahul.

Anima laughed and pinched Rahul's left ear. "This boy's tragic flaw is that he opens his mouth without thinking. And the poor thing always tells the truth. Know why?" Anima took Rahul's hand and spread his palm flat. "See here on his palm how the head line, heart line, and life lines all join together. Whatever's in his heart gets thought by his head, throwing his life into a tangle."

Anjali, Hemant, and Anima turned to examine their own palms; but either the head line was separate or all three lines were separate or only life and heart line were joined. None had all three lines intertwined. Hemant and Anjali both found this amusing.

"Have you shown this to an astrologer?" Anjali said, genuinely astonished.

"Yes," Rahul answered. "He said that according to the book of palmistry, a man with these lines becomes either a dictator, a fakir, he goes crazy or . . . it doesn't matter." Rahul stopped short.

"Oh, come on, tell us! Pleeeeeeease," she said, like a stubborn child.

"C'mon, yaar, let's have it. He'll go crazy or . . . ?" Hemant was excited.

Rahul thought about it for a second and then said, " . . . or he'll kill himself." His voice sounded like it was coming from underwater. Then, slowly and hoarsely, he added, "Like Sapam."

"Hey!" Anjali reproached, saying it so loudly that she felt embarrassed. Anima and Hemant both started laughing.

"Do you really believe in palmistry?" Hemant asked Rahul.

"No, I don't. They say Nehru had the same lines. Pandit

Jawaharlal Nehru. He wasn't crazy, or a fakir, and he didn't commit suicide," Rahul said.

"But a dictator, perhaps?' Hemant countered. "Otherwise how did his family rule India for so long?"

"In my opinion he did commit suicide—after the war with China," Rahul said.

"Look! Over there, here comes a camel," Anima pointed toward the hostel. Everyone looked. Coming toward them was a six-foot-three-inch-tall skeleton, skinny like a bamboo rod, bobbing at the neck with every step.

"Over here, skeleton boy! We were waiting for you," Rahul shouted.

O.P stopped halfway. "I'm going to go scrounge some snacks, yaar. I'm dying of hunger," he shouted from the road.

Both Rahul and Hemant were also hungry. The night before no food was served, in mourning for Sapam. Nothing today for breakfast, either. Their stomachs grumbled loudly.

"But the canteen's closed today. Where are you going to find food?" Anjali asked.

Hemant stood up. "Jang Bahadur lives in the yard behind the canteen. He'll hook us up."

Hemant walked off toward O.P., and Anima began to follow. "*Chalo*, I'll go with you. Maybe we'll get our hands on something . . ."

"Should I come along?" Anjali said, getting up.

"You two stay here. Discuss your Hindi literature. We'll be right back. See you, Anjali!" Anima smiled and winked. Anima, Hemant, and O.P. left for the canteen.

EIGHTEEN

Rahul and Anjali sat in the shadow of the neem tree. The yellow parasol that lay nearby trembled intermittently in the tiny gusts of wind. It seemed that if the wind blew just right, the parasol would spread its yellow wings with a start and take flight in the form of a butterfly.

A real butterfly, which had somewhere lost its way, fluttered by and landed for an instant on Anjali's shoulder.

"Shoo! Shoo!" Anjali leapt up, startled.

"What happened?" Rahul asked, concerned. The butterfly flew from Anjali's shoulder and hovered around the parasol before landing on its tip. What was amazing was that the butterfly shared the same yellow color as the parasol. A living, breathing, yellow, capable of flight, both alive and afraid. Fear made it fly from Anjali's shoulder.

"It's just a butterfly. What's there to be afraid of?" Rahul said, smiling at Anjali's alarm.

She sat down again in the grass. "What if it stings?" Anjali said.

"Butterflies don't sting."

"How do you know butterflies don't sting? What if this one did? Then what?"

"Butterflies don't sting," Rahul argued. "Bees do."

Anjali tried to put an end to the discussion, either to conceal her embarrassment or to avoid admitting she was wrong. "They're all the same, butterflies and bees."

"The same? What are you talking about? Butterflies never sting. Bees do—sometimes, anyway." Rahul clearly wasn't in the mood to quickly put the matter to rest.

"Have you ever been stung by a bee?" Anjali asked.

"Sure, a couple of times," Rahul said. "Back in the village, Papa built a big open tank next to the tube well in the field. We called it the hamam, and it was a lot of fun bathing in it during the summer."

"Did you ever go in?" Anjali asked.

"Of course. During summer vacation I'd run down there at night with a bar of soap and a towel and jump in. It was great fun. Even the soap had a strong scent there that it doesn't have here."

"How's that possible? Soap's the same everywhere."

"No, it's not. In the forest, near the fields, and at night, soap smells sweeter. It's true," Rahul said. "There were jasmine bushes growing next to the tank, and at night the blossoms smelled even more fragrant."

"What are you talking about?" Anjali was getting a bit irritated. "First you were talking about the sweet smell of soap, and now jasmine?"

"Oh! Well, if you ever go there, you'll see. When I swim there at night, the soap and jasmine both smell sweet. Sometimes I feel like I'm washing myself with jasmine instead of soap. And sometimes I could swear soap bushes are growing next to the tank. But since you've never swum there at night, how could you have any idea?" Rahul was also getting a bit irritated.

"But you were talking about bees. What do they have to do with all this?" Anjali looked at Rahul with slight displeasure.

"The bees are during the daytime. In the afternoon they hover around the water flowing near the tank—swarms of them. One afternoon when I went swimming, I hung my clothes and towel on the pipe of the tube well. A bee stung me when I started to dry myself off after I got out. They'd hidden in the towel."

Anjali started laughing hysterically.

"So you think that's funny? Wait till you get stung one day," Rahul said angrily.

"No, I don't. But I do wonder what would've happened if they'd hidden in your pants instead of the towel?"

Anjali started laughing again. Rahul watched. She was laughing so hard tears streamed from her eyes. How much laughter did this girl have inside her? As she laughed, her eyes remained fixed on Rahul. Suddenly he felt the same way he did gazing out the window of Room 252 in Tagore Hostel and watching the yellow spot bobbing along on the winding road from the field below.

Her laughing eyes floated into his insides, and Rahul felt them swim through the blood of his veins like two tiny shining fish. And in that red bloodstream, flowing in the darkness of his body's blue veins, they arrived at the place where all arteries and veins in the body join together. The place where the fragile and mysterious clock of life beats a continuous tick-tick, tick-tick. And the moment the ticking ceases, no more life! It's that place where the heart is.

A mild, pleasant fever crept over Rahul, the kind of feeling music can dissolve into. Rahul's ears heard the music within the fever and sank into it. What a melody—so faint he could hardly hear it, try as hard as he might. The two shining fish laughed and swam continuously inside his body, and back and forth across to the sweet fever.

"What happened?" Anjali said, waking Rahul from his reverie. "It's like you turned into a statue."

Rahul was silent. Sheepishly, he regarded Anjali. As if he were still seized by his fever, she still seemed to be laughing.

"Alright, alright. So, when was the second time you were stung by a bee?" Anjali asked.

"I was riding my motorcycle. I have no idea how but it got inside my helmet."

"My god! That's horrifying. A helmet strapped to your head with a bee trapped inside it," Anjali said, truly frightened.

"So then it stung me. I was so scared. I couldn't let go of the handlebars, and I couldn't take off my helmet . . ."

"So . . . so what did you do?" Anjali sounded worried.

"I nearly ran into an oncoming bus! If there'd been an accident, it would have been the bee's fault," Rahul said.

"My goodness!" Anjali said, reeling from the thought. "Then how did the bee get out of the helmet?"

"Get out? I pulled to the side, took the helmet off, and it just flew away."

"Oh!" Anjali let out a big sigh of relief. "Just thinking about it—how awful and scary it must have been to have a bee trapped inside your helmet buzzing around on your head."

"That's exactly how it was. And going fifty miles an hour on top of everything." Rahul smiled proudly.

But Anjali was no longer concerned. "You still haven't proven your point," she said.

"Huh?"

"The thing from before . . ."

"What thing?" Rahul didn't understand.

"The thing about butterflies not stinging," Anjali said.

Rahul started to laugh. "Butterflies don't sting. I'll bet you. Bees do, like I said."

"Just because bees sting doesn't mean that butterflies don't," Anjali argued.

"You're weird."

"Why?"

"Butterflies don't sting because they land on flowers. Bees, on the other hand, land on sweets and water near tanks," Rahul said. "Haven't you seen all the bees swarming in a sweets shop around the jalebis, the gujhi, the barfi?"

"Bees hover around flowers, and they sting. And flies swarm around sweets. They don't sting," Anjali countered.

Rahul was beginning to despair. How could he convince this girl that butterflies didn't sting? He'd been successful in convincing her that bees do. But that was only half a victory. Winning the other half was proving no easy task.

"Butterflies don't have stingers, so they don't sting. Bees have them. In the back, near the tail." Rahul argued his case with careful consideration as if playing his trump card.

Anjali raised another question: "Have you seen with your own eyes that there's no stinger on the back of the butterfly?"

Now Rahul gave up hope. He ran out of steam and fell flat on his back. His body went limp and he rolled around in the grass. "I give up! I now fully agree, Princess Diana-ji, that the butterfly that landed on your shoulder, flew off, and just landed on your parasol, stings. Okay? Happy? Can we please change the topic?"

Anjali began laughing again, maybe at her victory, maybe at Rahul's surrender.

"Now what's so funny?" Rahul's mood began to lighten as his annoyance abated.

Anjali grabbed a clump of grass with her right hand and tossed it at Rahul. "What is it with you? How do you manage to tell the truth, and still lose?" She laughed.

No one had said this to Rahul before. He felt as if Anjali, so easily, so casually, had managed to grasp this about him. This was the first time he and Anjali had quarreled, playfully, and even though he'd been right, he lost.

But why was this defeat feeling so good? Why was he so happy?

I drank
I drank
Now what? Now what?
My heart
Is hers
Now what? Now what?

Rahul began to hum the tune, slowly. There was shade under the neem tree. Thick and cool. A September breeze, filled with its afternoon freshness, moisture, and heat. The monsoon hadn't completely receded. Heavy clouds could gather in the sky at any moment and burst into rain.

The parasol was still in the same spot, occasionally trembling in the breeze. The butterfly on top had folded its wings and had, perhaps, fallen asleep.

Do butterflies dream? Rahul had read somewhere that we humans can perceive only seven of the colors in the spectrum, whereas butterflies can see thousands. Such a teeny-tiny flying insect with such beautiful wings. How small its eyes must be! And a retina smaller yet, the size of a pinprick. What kinds of tiny images would be created by a retina so small?

But images are nothing more than representations of light, read by the brain. So is the butterfly's brain, which senses thousands of symbols of color, more sophisticated than ours? And if that's the case, then the butterfly must also be capable of incredibly developed and sophisticated thought. This means the butterfly that flew, frightened, from Anjali's shoulder to the yellow parasol is now asleep, dreaming a Technicolor dream, magical, intricate, of a cosmos unknown.

If butterflies were capable of language, we could know about their dreams, colors, and world. Maybe they do have language and, just as we're not able to perceive the thousands of colors they can, we probably can't discern the various sounds, tones, and consonants of their sophisticaed, intricate, unknown tongue.

Butterflies would have their own alphabet if they could write. Who knows? The butterfly might be sitting on a flower or leaf and writing away. And wouldn't we be able to read it?

My goodness! More sophisticated than even the most complex computer filled with the best microchips is the brain of the butterfly. Who installed this biogenetic microchip inside the brain of this tiny insect? Who painted all the patterns on its wings?

"Is it really true?" Anjali asked. Her voice roused Rahul from his daze.

"Is what true?" he asked.

"The thing Anima mentioned the other day in the canteen."

"When?" Rahul played dumb.

"C'mon, don't you remember? Just after you got admission into the Hindi department and you were treating us to chai and samosas," Anjali said, in a serious attempt to stir his memory. However, there was absolutely no need to remind him.

"What are you talking about?" Rahul asked. "Don't beat around the bush."

Anjali thought about it for a moment and then haltingly began, "You know, the thing about dropping out of anthropology and transferring to the Hindi department because . . ."

Rahul studied Anjali. This was his chance to get revenge for the earlier defeat. "Because what?" he said innocently.

"Because . . ." Anjali said, glaring.

"Becaaauuuse?" Rahul asked again, drawing it out as far as he could.

"You're impossible!" She was annoyed. "Never mind. I don't care anyhow."

Anjali's remark stirred up something inside Rahul, and it was fear. Rahul felt that Anjali, even as she was asking him, was in no mood for jokes. She actually had been eager to find out why. But now the giggling was over and a kind of suffering and torment had begun. The lines of tension intersecting on her forehead were quite visible.

How beautiful those lines were, but why did they need to be there at all? Why did stress show up on the forehead of a girl who, ordinarily, was laughing? This too was because of him.

Rahul noticed that Anjali's eyes were fixed on him with an expression of eagerness or plea. There was something in her eyes that hadn't been there before.

Rahul felt his throat was dry, as if the sweet fever were again creeping up. He swallowed hard. His mouth was getting dry. He looked at Anjali and slowly said, "Yes."

"Yes what?" Anjali asked, her voice trembling.

"It's true," Rahul said. He lowered his head and ran his fingers over a blade of grass. Where had this sprouted from?

A cool breeze suddenly arrived. Even though it was September, the breeze retained some of August's leftover humidity. The blades of grass gently blew in the wind. A silence had descended.

Rahul lifted his head up; her eyes were as before, fixed on him. Rahul couldn't meet her gaze. He looked in the other direction, at the butterfly asleep atop the parasol rocking gently in the wind. The butterfly must certainly be dreaming now.

Right that instant, the magic began. Holding his breath and not blinking, Rahul's gaze fixed on the full expanse of that magic. There are twenty-four frames in each second of film. In slow motion he watched every instant and detail of whatever took place in that scene. It was surprising, amazing—Rahul could hardly breathe.

The butterfly, which had been sleeping, silently changed its form. A metamorphosis. It might not have even realized someone was watching this marvel. At least the butterfly was a living creature. But this marvel went so far that it even included the parasol—a lifeless thing made of fabric, plastic, and metal—in its magic. Now the parasol itself was silently changing its form.

Rahul was flabbergasted. It was the first time anything like this had happened to him, and right in front of his eyes. I'm awake, aren't I? He rubbed his eyes. So this is truly happening in reality?

The butterfly grew bigger and rounder. It grew larger with each passing instant, in each of the twenty-four frames for every second.

The parasol grew smaller at an identical rate. This meant that the butterfly and parasol were in cahoots, playing a game. They both knowingly participated in this act of magic. No more than thirty seconds could have elapsed by the time the butterfly had completely changed into the parasol and begun to flutter in the wind, as if it were the real parasol.

And the parasol had changed into a butterfly and was perched atop the parasol as if it were the real butterfly.

The color had drained from Rahul's face. He was dumbstruck. O god, what kind of jest is this!

Was this the dream the butterfly dreamed when it flew from Anjali's shoulder and fell asleep atop the parasol? Could it be that the thing Rahul saw was the butterfly's dream, occurring inside of its sleep? Or who's to say Rahul didn't have a quick nap and himself have a dream?

In the meantime he rubbed his eyes and saw clearly he was awake. Then he looked at Anjali. She was quite real, sitting in the same spot, eyes fixed on Rahul. Her gaze entered his pores, and Rahul felt it swim through the blood of his veins like tiny shining fish, swimming toward his heart, the place where the mysterious clock of life beats, tick-tick: the sound on which the whole of a life hangs.

This meant that the magic was real: the butterfly had really changed into a parasol and the parasol into a butterfly.

Just then, a leaf fell from the neem tree and floated down to the spot where the butterfly sat, which was, just a short while ago, actually a parasol. Frightened by the neem leaf, the butterfly took flight. But Rahul knew full well that it was not a butterfly at all, but a parasol.

"Look, the parasol's flying away," Rahul cried.

Anjali looked back to the ground, puzzled. "What are you talking about, it's right there," she said.

"No, that's a butterfly. *Believe me. It's a butterfly.*"

Anjali had a good laugh. "You really are a joker."

Rahul accepted defeat. He realized it would be nearly impossible to explain to this girl what had happened: the thing that just flew away was a parasol, and the thing still on the ground wasn't a parasol at all, but a butterfly.

"*Johnny joker, that's my name . . .*" Rahul said. In despair. These were the lyrics from a Shweta Shetty pop song.

Anjali looked at Rahul. This was the first time. Nothing needed to be said. It had happened, the thing that happens. Rahul felt as if a symphony inside him had begun to play for the first time.

Anima, O.P., and Hemant had returned. They brought cake, biscuits, a bag of Uncle Chipps, and five bottles of Pepsi.

"So did the two of you discuss Hindi literature?" Anima said, looking at Anjali. Anjali remained silent. Why did Anima's voice sound so flat and sorrowful?

When all who had gathered there began leaving, and Anjali had picked up her parasol, Rahul turned around and wanted to tell her the truth: it wasn't a parasol protecting her from the sun. It was actually a butterfly.

But he stayed silent and trailed behind the six-foot-three giraffe-like bamboo stick all the way back to the hostel and, once in the room, fell flat on the bed.

"I think I have fallen in love . . . for the first time in my life!" Rahul whispered into his pillow.

NINETEEN

Sapam's body still lay atop a slab of ice in the mortuary of Mahatma Gandhi Hospital waiting for either his father to retrieve him or to be shipped back home. The day of the month when the goondas normally attacked was drawing near. What a time it was.

Gopal Dwivedi said that S. N. Mishra, the senior professor of the Hindi department, was angry. He had said to Gopal he'd been wrong to secure admission for a certain student who had no business being there. The student was stirring up caste issues. Dr. Rajendra Trivedi and Dr. Loknath Tripathi said they always weed out such bad apples.

Parch them dry with not one drop, we'll hit and strike till dead they drop!

Rahul was face-to-face with a darkness that was closing in on him. But somewhere, far in the distance, he could make out the fluttering of a yellow butterfly. So even amid this anxiety, Rahul's lips were quick to trace the outline of a smile, and he fell asleep.

The eighth and ninth of September came and went. Meanwhile, Sapam's body had been shipped to Imphal by train. Kartikeya, Madhusudan, Pratap, Masood, Praveen, O.P., and some twenty-five students, among them girls, too, presented Vice-Chancellor Agnihotri with a petition in which they demanded

Sapam's body be returned to Imphal by airplane and that the culprits responsible for robbing and beating him be arrested.

Regarding the latter demand, the vice-chancellor gave the students the assurance that he would liaise with the police, but as far as sending the body back to Manipur by air, he continued, there simply was not enough money in the University Welfare Fund.

During the same period, a meeting of the SMTF was held in Praveen's room. The core committee member students of the Special Militant Task Force from the four hostels (Arbind, Raman, Tagore, and Desai) decided to link the hostels by a restricted frequency radio transmission. The total expenditure was only 800 rupees, which, through donations, was collected in under three hours. Hemant, Madhusudan, and Praveen teamed up to install speakers in designated rooms in each of the four hostels. Pratap, Kartikeya, and Rahul procured three microphones. It took three run-throughs to ensure that when the time came the students would be ready for action in less than ten minutes. They also collected data on which students expected money orders or had received them, and for how much, for all four hostels. These were the students the goondas usually targeted—those who were receiving the most money.

D. Gopal Rajulu, Akhilesh Ranjan, and Naukant Jha—these three students topped the list. Winter was approaching, and their families had sent them additional funds to buy warm clothing. Gopal Rajulu's brother was a doctor. For years Rajulu had wanted to buy a camera. He was going on a bus tour to Calcutta, and before he left his brother in Virginia wanted him to have 20,000 rupees.

At the top of the hit list was D. Gopal Rajulu. Number two: Akhilesh Ranjan. Number three: Naukant Jha. Three students, one from Andhra Pradesh and two from Bihar.

But during this period of time Anjali was everywhere, too!

TWENTY

The days were largely filled with the kind of bankrupt happenings found on the pages of a third-rate dime store romance or in the usual Bollywood fare. The main storyline's sequence of events had no rhyme or reason, filled with all manner of coincidence and happenstance. Absurd, sophomoric, and cheap—yet thrilling. Sex, violence, glamour, intrigue, obscenity, special effects, tears, screams, and heartwarming situations, all laced with song.

The screenplay for this snapshot of time seems to have been written by a sensitive gambler; each time he makes a new move in the plot, he immediately fears its consequences.

But during this period something else was happening—something as beautiful, cool, and pure as drops of morning dew falling from a leaf.

As Rahul emerged from the classroom into the corridor, someone snuck up from behind and bumped into him. Rahul turned around to look—it was Anjali, with her laugh.

In the library, Rahul was hunched over a desk, taking some notes, when suddenly someone blew into his ear—*pffffff!*—so intense it sent shivers up his spine. It was Anjali.

Rahul was taking a walk when a cold, pointy thing jabbed him in the neck. He turned around. Anjali was standing there, laugh-

ing, holding the closed parasol, the tip pointed at him—en garde!
—trying to frighten him.

Back in the library, looking at books in the narrow space
between the shelves, someone's shoulder gave him a little shove. It
was Anjali's.

Rahul was on his way to the canteen with Shailendra George
and Shaligaram. Anjali was coming the other way with Chandra,
Shuba Mishra, and Sharmishtha. The infamous gang of no-good
locals stood just a few feet away, on the side of the road. With them
was Lakkhu, the one who'd thrown a rock that day first at Rahul
and then at Abha. "Your mother!" Rahul was afraid one of them
might start something again. "O hero! If we get ahold of you, we'll
turn you from Rahul Rai into Anupam Kher, not a blade of hair
left on your head!" Anjali had peeled off from her group and was
coming in toward Rahul, eyes on him. The same smiling eyes
transformed into two tiny shining fish, at once swimming in his
bloodstream.

As the two groups crossed paths, Anjali suddenly tripped and
stumbled to the side. It seemed the heel of her sandal had caught a
rock and she'd slipped, but her stumble was quite fake and deliberate; in the middle of it she managed a quick pinch of Rahul's back,
holding it for a moment. An "ouch!" came from Rahul's mouth. In
his ear he heard the word "bee."

A clever bird had played her own little trick before the cunning eyes of a gang of hunting hawks. She returned to her own
group, now laughing at something else.

Oh! You are so brilliant. This is why I love you. I'm just a
dumb donkey, but you, madam, one day you can hop on my back

and I'll carry you to the moon. I promise! Have you ever heard a
donkey sing?

My heart cries out
From choppy seas
Hear me, love!
Hear me, please!

If Hemant Barua, Kartikeya, or O.P. had been there, they
would've guessed immediately that "something" had happened.
But Rahul was with his two first-year Hindi MA friends. Shaligaram said, "Rahul-ji, you've really got a lovely voice, and you
sing so well."

"Oh! Please, it was nothing, it just came out," Rahul said,
blushing.

Anjali was on the lookout these days for any excuse to touch
Rahul. And Rahul was taking part in the same plot.

Anjali was coming out of class to go to lunch with the other
girls. Rahul stealthily managed to squeeze her pinkie. The first
time in the library he gave her ponytail a little tug, the second time
he pinched her ear, the third time he lightly placed his hand on
her waist, and the fourth time, for a few seconds, her took her hand
in his.

This was a new language, which Rahul and Anjali were being
exposed to for the first time. Sentences in this language were
different, its syntax unique. Each day they slowly learned something new about its particular grammar. The lessons were full of
such wonder, eagerness, joy, and an impatience that took their

breath away, that each one left them speechless, drained, numb. The experience cloaked their sense of self with a kind of sorcery that made them feel as if in all of creation, they two were alone.

There were words in this language that weren't articulated with sound. They had no need for an alphabet, or even letters to write. This was the kind of language that functioned by electricity and magnetic waves. Electromagnetic current. It was possible to express anything in this language merely by touching one another. And when they did their bodies became paralyzed, caught in a whirlwind, a whitewater of enchanted energy, like blades of grass blown in the wind, helpless.

That day in the library, for example, in the tiny, narrow space between the bookshelves, surrounded by dank and dusty smells, Rahul took Anjali's hand in his, which sparked a turbulent electromagnetic storm inside his body and radiated such an eruption of feeling, that, without a word being spoken, Rahul could see how it heated Anjali's fair-colored face to a hot dirty copper. Her eyes seemed filled with submissiveness, and it seemed she might faint onto the floor. He himself felt that the blood in his veins had abandoned its molten form and changed to vapor or raw energy, and Anjali's hand in an instant drank him up. His knees were shaking. He'd become void of power, quivering like a weak plant in a violent storm.

Could there really be something to "Reiki," which Rahul had never believed in? The Japanese therapy of touch, which is said to have to have been brought to Japan from India centuries ago by Buddhist monks. He who loves becomes a Buddhist monk. And whoever he touches is cured of all that ails. Someday I'll heal you

and someday you too can heal me—if you please! Because you too
are a Buddhist she-monk. *Right?*

How strange was that moment, when in less than thirty seconds a butterfly, through a singular act of magic, assumed the form
of a parasol, and now the butterfly, casting a spell over the whole
world, had brought Rahul's sense of his own existence under its
wing.

And during that time, the greedy, potbellied, gluttonous, rich,
lustful, corrupt, depraved, fat man was present still, armed with his
marketplace and his power. And even those awful "critters" had
smeared blood on every tract of reality with their violence, plun-
der, immorality, and transgression.

The worrying thing was that a frighteningly large number of
"critters" were also present within another language, the language
that Rahul, after dropping anthropology, had hitched his star to,
and, what's more, a language they've seized control of. Namely,
Hindi.

TWENTY-ONE

The night of September the twelfth. Ten thirteen and twenty-three seconds.

Kartikeya Kajle's voice echoed over the speakers in the rooms in the four boys' hostels where the core committee members of the SMTF lived. "Hello! Hello! Get ready. Quick. The jeep's in the gate of C. V. Raman Hostel. Get hold of everything you have! Okay—wait for the next call. Okay. Over and out."

As fast as they could, Niketan, Praveen, Masood, Madhusudan, Kannan, O.P., Ravi, Dinesh, Imroz, Parvez, Hemant Barua, Dinamani, Ramesh Ataluri, Gulab Kesavani, and the rest of the twenty-five boys from the four hostels armed themselves with hockey sticks, iron rods, knives, dandas, Rampuri knives, switch-blades, chains, and homemade pistols. Other students ran back and forth as fast as they could from one end of the hostel to the other to spread the information to the other students. Some scaled to the roof of C. V. Raman Hostel carrying Molotov cocktails, bricks, stones, and hand grenades. The goondas' jeep was idling below.

D. Gopal Rajulu: Room 112. Naukant Jha: Room 148. These two students, from Andhra Pradesh and Bihar, living in C. V. Raman Hostel, were on the top of the hit list. Rajulu had received a money order for 20,000 rupees and Naukant Jha one for 8,500.

The bald, shrewd, decrepit postman, growing old, had spied

again, greedy for commission. But the difference this time was the students had intercepted his information and were ready before the criminals could make their move.

Twenty minutes later, the SMTF swung into action.

Bang, bang, bang!

The door of Room 112 was kicked in and a group of boys barged into Rajulu's room like a whirlwind. At that very instant, the main circuit breaker was thrown and all four hostels were plunged into darkness.

Biff! Bam! Whiz!

In the dark, billy clubs, rods, and hockey sticks went into motion. A sudden crashing sound from somewhere. Someone fired a pistol. Glass was breaking.

Lacchu Guru, the notorious town goonda with a police record a mile long, lay writhing on the ground of Room 112 with his four underlings, covered in blood. He had been relieved of his pistol. He'd sustained fifty blows in under a minute.

The five goondas were in a state of shock. They were being dragged into the hallway.

"Be careful. We don't want them to die. Take them downstairs . . ." Rahul was issuing instructions. His beefed-up arms were pulsating. The six-foot-three skinny skeleton O.P., center forward on the field, was using his hockey stick to score a few more goals on Lacchu Guru's skull. Pratap and Kartikeya looked dead serious.

Eighteen-year-old first-year Niketan, who hardly had a trace of facial hair, had transformed into Bruce Lee and was in the middle of the goondas lashing them with his belt like a whip.

The main circuit breaker was switched back on. A simultaneous chorus ushered from all four hostels. "Ho! Ho! Hurray! The electricity's back!"

It had been a first-rate success. In their eagerness, some of the students wanted to torch the goondas' jeep, and had even poured gasoline on it. It came so close they were ready to toss a Molotov cocktail down from the roof, or light a match. But Pratap and Masood talked them out of it. Nevertheless, this didn't mean that the goondas would be able to make a getaway in their jeep; to make sure they didn't, the air had been let out of all four tires.

The goondas were marched down the steps down to the field in front of Raman Hostel. More than three hundred students had materialized in a flash. Their faces beamed with the pride of the victorious and delight in their success.

"Hip, hip, hooray!"

Hip hip hip hip.

"Down with goondas!"

"No more goondas!"

Ajay Devgan took a giant leap from somewhere in the crowd and landed both his boots on the goondas' backs, just like Bruce Lee, shouting "ho, shu, shu," showing off his karate-judo moves, whipping his belt around in the air. He removed his shirt with the bloodthirsty look of Arnold Schwarzenegger in *Terminator* and, grabbing the bewildered goondas by the scruff of their necks, hoisted them in the air, just as a massive monkey arrived on the scene and used his bare fist to rain blow after blow on the goondas' ugly mugs. The chant of victory echoed from the crowd—"Victory to Hanuman!"

Rahul, as Pierce Brosnan of James Bond fame, pretended to

help Lacchu Ustad to his feet while simultaneously kicking his legs out from under him, then laughed deeply.

And in the middle of the chaos emerged Johnny Lever and Jim Carrey from *Mask,* as the two clowning jokers flashed their teeth and began leaping around in song—

Shall I kill you, or let you go—speak . . .

and

I am the Don, I am the Don . . .

The six-foot-three ostrich became the superstar Amitabh Bachan, dancing away, kicking his sticklike legs into the air.

"*Ab tera kya hoga re, Kaliyaa?* Looks like the end of the line!" Gabbar Singh and Sambha said to the cowering, blood-soaked goondas.

Someone placed his hand on Rahul's shoulder. It was Dinamani. He'd come from Manipur to do a postgraduate degree in geology. "He's the one! Now I can make it out. He's the one who beat Sapam. I recognize him. It's 100 percent confirmed, I tell you!"

O.P. and Kartikeya had to restrain Rahul. He resisted like a wounded leopard, trying to break free. "I'll kill him!"

"Control! Control yourself, Rahul! Rahul!" Kartikeya screamed.

The goondas were loaded into the back of the jeep. Students took up every inch of remaining space, from the hood in front to the spare tire in the back. The jeep, with no air in its tires, set off very slowly toward the residence of Vice-Chancellor Ashok Kumar Agnihotri, trailed by the throng of students.

Rahul noticed that amid the crowd of hooting and hollering students following the jeep were Sapam and his brother, walking silently. Rahul's eyes met Sapam's for an instant, and he saw Sapam's brother. Blood still flowed from his temple. It was the spot on his head where the police, thinking him a terrorist, had shot him dead while he was on his way to school to teach.

"Every civilization absolutely needs to have a big collective dream, a utopian ideal, one without self-interest. History has shown us that there hasn't been any civilization without some sort of craze or madness," Kinnu Da had once said.

"Have you read Michel Foucault? The fear and avarice in the West toward lepers and nonwhite indigenous peoples in the fifteenth and sixteenth centuries was nothing more than a craze, a frenzy, a collective neurotic disorder. The notion that ideas, religions, philosophies, and political theories are great ones, or worthless ones, depends on the kind of utopia or frenzy or dream they manage to create in the minds of the individuals of that civilization, and to what extent they contain a minimal degree of violence, hatred, fear, and destruction. Buddha and Gandhi were so remarkable because there was no place in their dreams for violence or hatred. Meanwhile, most of the 'constructs' that have issued forth from the West have not been fully devoid of violence or hatred."

Kinnu Da's voice echoed in Rahul's ears. "Rahul, the West has beaten Gandhi for good. My fear is that soon we'll have a bloodbath and everything will be broken up into tiny pieces."

Rahul looked at Sapam and his brother. Then he saw the great master, Chaitanya, mortally wounded, standing beneath the neem tree along with his broken drum and cymbals. Then he saw that a map of the country he loved with all his heart was breaking into tiny pieces, scattering, and disappearing into a black hole.

"I'm not opposed to the market. But the market is no 'collective dream,' no utopia. No dream can be seen in the marketplace. There is nothing in it that is great, moral, or lofty. All its ingredients—gains, losses, profit, cash—are tiny and base. The market is operated by the science of exploitation, greed, gambling, thuggery, and self-interest." Kinnu Da's voice was grave and sad. "Can't you see with your own eyes that wherever a market comes to a country, the place is torn to bits and handed over to violence and bloodshed."

The great countries and united republics—those that had been eaten away by market forces—flashed before Rahul's eyes: Kosovo, Serbia, Yugoslavia, the Soviet Union.

America and some rich European countries had become countries of commerce, and then transformed third world societies into their wholesale markets, turning them on their heads, bringing destruction and violence, flooding them with their brokers. The limbs were dismembered and organs ripped from one society after another, from one once-sovereign country to another, and then brought into conflict. Scattered, wasted, spoiled.

It's interesting that television and newspapers only report the daily ups and downs of the stock market index, but not the nonstop destruction, disintegration, violence, and conflict happening everywhere, from all sides, twenty-four hours a day.

Now is it our turn? Who is the agent representing this market? Who is the real enemy of the country? Is it the offspring of the demon Ravana, cast across the ocean by Pulastya? Have they returned, the English having, in fact, handed over power to them?

Rahul, O.P., Kartikeya, Parvez, Imroz, and Hemant were standing together on the back of the jeep. Their hands were clasped together and they sang:

Let the time come, O heavens, and we'll tell
But for now in our hearts—what can we say?
Sacrifice, sacrifice—the longing for sacrifice

Vice-Chancellor Ashok Kumar Agnihotri, after a long period of slogan chanting by the students, finally emerged from his residence. He'd called the police. Soon they arrived and took away Lacchu Guru and his four wounded associates.

He promised that the university would beef up security in the student hostels. The students shouldn't take the law into their own hands. He had information that weapons had been stockpiled in some students' rooms. This was illegal. He'd used his influence to dissuade the superintendent of police, who otherwise would have already raided and searched several rooms in the hostel.

The VC added he'd also received information about the indecent conduct of a few students. Students should focus their entire concentration on building their futures. If you asked him, he was against the type of higher education that was unrelated to the question of job salary or earning potential. We are living through such wonderful times, with endless career opportunities. Short-term courses were now offered. Why waste your time with dead-end pursuits? *Take a diploma and fly to America*, the vice-chancellor advised with a laugh.

"Sir, the criminals that were just now apprehended were exactly those ones who beat Sapam Tomba within an inch of his life . . ."

"They tried to sodomize him . . . and they made him urinate on the heater and it was the shock from that which . . ."

Rahul and Dinamani tried to interrupt the VC. "Sir, the Sapam Tomba who committed suicide!"

"Oh!" Ashok Agnihotri exclaimed, his tone turning serious. "*I will look into it.* What a tragedy. I have a lot of sympathy for his father. Poor chap . . . I called the governor and chief secretary of Manipur. They had his father informed. You know, that's why the fashion show and cultural program of September 10 was postponed. Because of it, the university took an 800,000-rupee loss. We've talked with the sponsors. It would have been an excellent source of revenue. I had made such grand plans. I realized we need to generate extra funds on our own. What does the UGC give us? Everything goes to staff salaries. I want to develop a park here. I want to computerize the entire administration. I want to provide twenty-four-hour net-surfing access in all student hostels, for a nominal and reasonable fee."

"Your security officers are mixed up with the local goondas and criminals, sir!"

"And the postman tells all of them which students are getting how much money sent . . ."

"The hostel warden is bungling the job terribly, sir!"

"There's rampant cheating in the admission process, sir!"

"The dining hall food's not even fit for a dog, sir!"

"There's no doctor and no medicine in the dispensary . . ."

"The Hindi department's a den of Brahmanists, sir."

"Teachers don't teach classes and are always on strike. It's a big loss for students, sir!"

Everyone watched as the smile from Agnihotri's face suddenly disappeared, replaced by anger and annoyance. He marched back inside his bungalow with his four security guards.

Back in the Max Cyber Cafe, information about Vice-Chancellor Ashok Agnihotri was fed into the de facto file and came out like this:

> The Vice-Chancellor is so technically dexterous and cunning in constructing a web of fiscal duplicity and abusing monetary funds to suit his purposes that there is no chance he'll be caught for his corruption. During his tenure as VC he's promoted only his yes-men, family members, and love interests. Ignoring wholesale the rules and regulations of the University Grants Commission, and without advertising the positions, Mr. Ashok Agnihotri appointed his flunkeys and in-laws, who had no proper academic qualifications, to various posts, totally at his whim, and then put them in charge of various projects, awarded them grants and fellowships, and sent them abroad. The person whom Agnihotri appointed as editor of the English list of the university press had a degree in Hindi, and couldn't write a complete sentence in English. An individual made professor of psychology had received his degree from Pantnagar Technical Community College in horticulture. The new professor of mathematics had been in the

bottom third of his graduating class in botany. But despite all this, no one dared open their mouths to speak against Agnihotri because most of them were greedy, cunning cohorts who'd been pressed into compliance by Agnihotri's favors. Another main power base of his derived from the deep connections and caste ties he maintained inside the range of educational institutions and cultural foundations. To mark the occasion of his sixtieth birthday, a local institution used university money to publish a special commemorative volume on Agnihotri in which testimonials from twenty-eight writers —twenty-one Brahmins, three Baniyas, one Kayastha, two Thakurs, and one foreigner—proved that his fame had spread more widely throughout the world than even that of Emperor Ashoka, Akbar the Great, or Alexander.

According to the de facto file, he'd received a nice commission from a secret deal to lease a few hundred acres of university land to some local real estate developers and businessmen. He considers university funds to be his own private bank account, and to drink a glass of water he goes to London, and to piss he goes to America. This corrupt vicechancellor is allowed to be so powerful because the system itself is corrupt through and through.

Kartikeya Kajle said, "Look, if nothing is done, this country will turn into another Haiti, Panama, Colombia, or Dubai. The Mafia Raj will take over, and come Gandhi's birthday on October 2, they'll be the only ones permitted at Rajghat. All other citizens will not be allowed to enter."

"Why are you talking about this in the future tense?" Pratap said, laughing. "It's already happened, or about to." Pratap may have been joking, but a sense of real distress hid behind the laughter. The darkness of the days to come flashed before his eyes.

"I've been thinking," O.P. said. "Maybe I should throw myself at the feet of the vice-chancellor, wrap my arms around his ankles, and say, 'O invincible Satan of our times, I rub my nose on the soles of your feet and beseech you to find a place for me just as you've found a place for your lapdogs and concubines.' I'm scared, Rahul!" he said. He was always laughing and garrulous. But the dark shadow of despair and defeat crept into his voice.

Rahul, Hemant, O.P., Kartikeya, Praveen, Niketan, Parvez, Imroz, Masood, Ramesh Ataluri, Dinamani, Ravi, Madhusudan— all of these young men, age eighteen to twenty-four, had come here to study from various states, towns, and villages all over the country. Their parents weren't the big businessmen, real estate developers, property agents, middlemen, or corrupt bureaucrats who trafficked in undeclared black money and lived in big metropolitan cities like Delhi-Bangalore-Chennai-Calcutta, but rather came from honest, hardworking families of farmers, small businessmen, and low-grade civil servants. Every month they'd cut corners and borrow money from somewhere so they could send money to their children, money steeped in their families' tears, sweat, and dreams.

These weren't the people seen with great regularity on TV and in newspapers. When they watched the colorful, well-off Indian Middle Class on TV, with their living room, dining room, terrace, car in garage, cell phone in hand—their eyes nearly popped out of their sockets. Meanwhile, the plaster is peeling off the walls, the roof is cracked, the doors creak, the dal needs to be cleaned and cooked and flour kneaded into roti for lunch or dinner, all the while calculating the ever-rising cost of living, and interest on the money they've borrowed. Without dowry, their daughters remain at home, unmarried, and their sons, unemployed, are so ashamed they stay away from the house all day long. These sons can be found in groups hanging around railway platforms, standing on the side of the road, sitting near cramped workmen's quarters or in a storefront with a public payphone or in some vacant, empty place, lost in wait for a miracle.

These young men numbered tens of millions. They were not defective in either body or mind. They were young men full of limitless capability, talent, and hard work. But worry had made their cheekbones protrude.

"I'll make a million somehow and really show those sister-fuckers . . ."

"I haven't gone home in three days. The old man's started counting the roti I eat. Got any money? Can you fix us up with some chai . . ."

"You know that big finance guy, T. D. Gupta. The fat, macho bastard's looking to settle down and he's got his eyes on my sister. Last month she got a job, 800 rupees a month."

"Kundanani was saying, one trip to Singapore means 10,000 for me."

"And he'll fuck you if you get caught. Is his papa gonna pay your bail?"

"Yaar, if I could just get my hands on Rajan or Ibrahim's phone number . . ."

"5,000, that's all I'm asking for, and I swear, I'd kill anyone."

"Ramashankar took himself a trip to Nepal and made out like a bandit. He was talking about taking me along next time."

"That Deepa, you know, the Khaddus Bakery daughter? Ever since she opened that beauty parlor, her parents' luck totally turned around . . ."

"Beauty parlor my ass. That's just a cover for another hobby of hers. Junior engineer Sharma and builder Satvinder are both in on it, and in on her . . ."

"Don't let her brother hear that. He'll fix your clock."

"Let him hear, the little bastard. He's just a commission man. Give me 2,000 and I can take you over to see her right now."

"Hey, Kishore, didn't you do an MSc in Physics?"

"Yeah, but I've forgotten fucking everything. Now I think I'll get into politics. Listen, I've got a plan. I'll get some fake papers to make it look like I have a job, show them to some lucky parents, get married with a big dowry, have a humping week-long honeymoon, sell the wife, and take off for Dubai. God knows, I'm sick of this kind of life."

The Indian markets were crammed full of every kind of perfume, cosmetic, soft drink, electronic gadget, washing machine, cell phone, digital TV, and handicam. Every week half a dozen new car models were coming out. In Delhi, hundreds of fast-food joints like McDonalds, KFC, and Nirulas were opening their doors. Nightclubs were sprouting up in the capital and in other big cities, where half-naked models served whiskey and wine, and the children of ministers, government bureaucrats, and criminals were having great fun. Indian and non-Indian lottery games operated openly, addicting people to them and dangling dreams of becoming millionaires and billionaires in front of their faces. The amount of money that ministers and government bureaucrats of this country spend on lunch in one day could bring drinking water, schoolteachers, and blackboards to all the villages in India, bring electricity to fields and homes, and be used to install proper toilets for slum dwellers.

But every person who thinks along those lines is considered to be a backward, out-of-step, old-fashioned stuffed ape in a museum. Every person with such ideas will be given a swift kick by the system, which will then shove him into the junkyard or label him a dangerous lunatic, and try to destroy him by any and all means.

The Parliament of India has been filled with killers, smugglers, lackeys of foreign companies, profiteers, black marketeers—all dishonest. Five-star hotels bloomed like flowers. Rivers of booze flowed through them. Mountains, forests, rivers, fields, minerals, ore, women, children, historical moments, conscience, religion, air, water, oceans: everything was being auctioned off. The prime minister was going to jail. Embezzlement, corruption, and thuggery cases were pending against multiple state chief ministers. The judge was on the take. Police were in cahoots with criminals, and each day of the turn of the century was smeared with the blood of innocent, honest, justice-seeking Indians.

One Jallianwallah Bagh massacre occurred at the hands of the English; now, dozens of Jallianwallah Baghs happen every day.

The bastard offspring of Ravana have hoisted the flag of Ram and consolidated their control over every facet of reality.

Not a moment of peace, my friend
Not a moment of rest, my friend
And no end in sight

The boys waiting for a miracle were singing. Their faces sank into a dark shadow that grew more thick and dense with each passing moment. The night was so late, the darkness so dark, the silence so silent that it was terrifying.

Yet, on some leaf in this time of desolation and waste fell drops of cool dew, clear and uncorrupted, whose moistness still, occasionally, greened life.

TWENTY-TWO

Dr. Rajendra Tiwari's class was over. He'd been lecturing about the poet Vidyapati. With half-closed, lust-filled eyes, he'd been explaining the "meanings" of words like *bosom, teat, loin*, and *fornication*. To him, it seemed, women equaled bosoms, teats, loins, and the three auspicious folds of the belly. The girls in class stared at the floor. The boys—Balram Pandey, Vijay Pachauri, Vimal Shukla, and Vibhuti Prasad Mishra—winked and smiled at one another.

Because of his connections through his brother-in-law, who was a member of the Rajya Sabha, Dr. Rajendra Tiwari had been awarded a prestigious Indian government Padmashree award. Among the professor's habits were gawking at female students, spying on them in the library, and phoning their parents. He'd been beaten up twice for it. His favorite pastime was having big conferences organized in his honor in various cities and towns. He was famous for carrying a bag containing a shawl, a coconut, an envelope with 501 rupees, and a framed, printed certificate of appreciation wherever he went. The local headlines would read, "Special Function Held in City to Honor Renowned Hindi Scholar Dr. Rajendra Tiwari." Every fortnight he would receive an award or prize, for which he had personally made the arrangements. The title of his PhD dissertation was "Erotic Sentiment in Krishna Poetry," but no one had ever seen it.

The girls stood in the door to the classroom. Rahul, Shailendra George, and Shaligaram were leaving for the library. They needed to check out some books. As he passed her, Rahul touched Anjali's elbow. She looked at him and began to follow behind with Sharmistha toward the library.

At the steps of the library, Anjali called out to him, "Rahul! Come here for a second!"

Rahul approached her.

"I need to talk with you," she said.

"Now?"

"No. Tomorrow morning, I'll come early."

"What time?" Rahul's heart started racing. Anjali's face looked as if it'd been licked by the flames of fever.

"Eight thirty," Anjali said, voice trembling.

"Done! I'll be waiting," Rahul said before running off to the library, where Shaligaram and Shailendra were standing at the circulation desk.

Rahul requested three books, *The History of Hindi Literature*, by Professor Ramchandra Shukla, *Anamdas ka Potha*, by Hazariprasad Dwivedi, and *The Collected Works of Nirala*, which contained the poem "How Rama Worshipped Shakti."

As he left the library on his way back to the department, he thought for a moment, why are all three authors Brahmins?

And Anjali? Daughter of the state minister for the Public Works Department L. K. Joshi? She too, no?

What a paradox, thought Rahul, that the caste determined to eradicate him and countless others like him, whose immoral, unjust, and corrupt conduct has stretched this moment in time to the breaking point, is the same caste that claims among its numbers the writers whose works he's reading, and a certain girl who pulses inside each and every tick of his heartbeat.

Who has power over my heart and mind? Who rules my thoughts and deeds, and who controls my perceptions? The language in which I speak, write, and think is under the authority of whom?

O bastard offspring of Ravana, cackling through the centuries, seizer of socioeconomic power, head of the caste system, I truly don't know whether I love you or hate you!

Rahul was struck numb. A strange battle was being waged inside him, like the process in which an antibiotic, injected into the bloodstream, fights the disease-causing bacteria by giving birth to the same microbe, in the same body. His own brain had become a hellhole and host of a bitter struggle. The struggle in his blood between disease and treatment, affliction and cure, was fearsome.

Rahul opened *The Collected Works of Nirala* and began reading:

Oh night of deep silence! The heavens vomit darkness;
all sense of direction lost, even the wind's flow stilled;
thundering behind them the vast unconquerable sea;
the mountains as thought plunged in thought, only one
        torch burning.
Again and again doubt rocks Lord Rama, and gradually
with the dread of Ravana's victory in the universe . . .

These lines were from the poem "How Rama Worshipped Shakti." Rahul, strangely, had opened the book to find that particular poem right in front of his face.

So? It means that . . . there is someone, observing this struggle being waged in my consciousness. Silently. Invisibly. Thank you . . . thank you. A cool gust of wind came from the direction of the neem tree, providing Rahul with a sense of peace.

"What happened, Rahul-ji? Are you lost somewhere?" Shaligaram said.

Rahul put his hand on Shailendra George's shoulder and said, laughing, "No, Shaligaram-ji, *I've been swept away with the feeling . . . ki kariye, ki kariye.*"

"You're a funny one, yaar Rahul brother!" Shailandra George said, placing his arm around Rahul's shoulder.

TWENTY-THREE

In the morning, Rahul stood next to the window in Room 252 brushing his teeth. It was barely seven thirty. O.P. was showering in the bathroom. Rahul stared out at the winding road that ran alongside the playground below.

The yellow meandered its way up from the residential development. Rahul, startled, looked over to the clock on the wall: seven thirty-two. What had happened? She was supposed to come at eight thirty.

Rahul wiped the window with his hand and looked carefully. It was the same yellow butterfly from the other day that had changed into a parasol. There was no doubt, none at all. The blood in his veins picked up pace. Desire seized him. The sound of his throbbing heart went straight to his ears. Tick . . . Tick . . .

The words tumbled out of his mouth: "That's the one! I'm sure of it." He jumped right into his pants, dried his face with a towel, threw on his shoes, and ran out, leaping down the stairs three at a time.

Anjali absolutely glowed—she wore a white salwar with a scattershot-dotted almond and light green kurta. Her chunni was light green. Her hair was clean and shiny, blowing every which way with each gust of wind.

She spotted Rahul. "Jeez! How did you know I was here? You're completely out of breath!"

"I was standing at the window of my room."

"So that's where you're posted these days, standing at your window?" Anjali asked, looking around. She seemed a little nervous. The morning sun shone far off in the distance; the grass on the playground was still moist with dew.

"Can we cut through the park instead of going by road?" Rahul asked, touching Anjali's elbow. "And weren't you coming at eight thirty?" he added, slowly sidling up to her. He inhaled deeply the sweet fragrance of her body and clothing.

"I was getting bored. Papa's never around since the state assembly is in session. My brother stays up until three in the morning and then sleeps until noon."

"Do you ever think about me? Even sometimes?" Rahul touched her arms.

Anjali stopped. Her eyes were timid and anguished. She looked at Rahul as if expecting his insides to react to her distress. "Why just sometimes?" She fell silent for a moment as if she were searching for her lost voice. "Each and every moment, Rahul!"

Rahul's insides jumped. He was seized by that sweet fever, penetrated by deep desire, one barely audible to the ears. Why was this? Rahul thought. Why was it that the moment he neared Anjali, or saw Anjali, the mysterious churning began inside his body, like some kind of chemical reaction, slowly encasing his sense of being, taking his breath away; why was it he'd never felt like this before?

This life belongs to me. So how did it change itself without my consent?

Rahul thought, I'd wanted to pump myself up in the gym until I became a cheetah or sleek panther, ready to pounce on my prey. So who was that Shahrukh who bloodied the girl he fell in love with? He raped her. Called her on the phone, frightened her. I thought girls went for this sort of guy, the violent kind who leaves scars. But between Anjali and me there's nothing but butterflies and parasols. On TV you see a woman in a bathing suit lounging on a beach under a palm tree, wearing sunglasses, arm around the waist of her man—that feeling must be the same as I'm feeling for Anjali, no?

Rahul looked at Anjali. And she looked at him. He took Anjali's right hand into his. And that was that. He immediately felt the electromagnetic storm begin to surge through his body. Anjali's face reflected the morning sunlight, giving it a dusky copper color. Now the storm had become an inescapable whirlwind that caught Rahul like a helpless stalk of grass, unbound.

"Should we go over there?" Rahul suggested. At the base of the hill leading up to the hostel were huge rocks, the ground covered with semal and babul trees, sirkin and lentina shrubs. There was a small storeroom tucked away where sports equipment was kept. It was always locked. Behind it were more bushes, and no one.

Rahul brushed aside the strands of hair that had fallen in Anjali's face. For the first time, she gave Rahul's hand a tight squeeze, with all her strength. Then she smiled at him.

"That's all you've got?" Rahul teased. "Want to hand wrestle?"

"You're on!" Anjali linked her fingers into Rahul's hand and tried to overpower him. Oh! How far away this girl had once been. Walking underneath her yellow parasol. Eating roast corn that day, totally absorbed.

Rahul pulled her toward him after she'd given up and let go, nearly falling. In a deserted area behind the field storage, in a small space between a few big rocks and lentina bushes, Anjali's and Rahul's lips madly began exploring each other's faces. The only sound was of hot breath.

The butterfly that had fooled the whole world by turning into a parasol was now visited by another butterfly, which fluttered down and sat atop it, and, perhaps guessing the secret that it wasn't a parasol, but really just a butterfly, decided to whisper something in its ear in its own language.

Rahul and Anjali had planted so many kisses on one another's faces that they'd become moist and sticky. They could hardly catch their breath. Passion, distress, and restlessness all mixed in their eyes.

"I love you, Anjali," Rahul managed to say, his voice choked. He wanted to hear the same words from Anjali, but she was silent. Totally quiet. Rahul once again pressed his lips to her face.

Anjali took Rahul's right hand and traced the words in his palm: "I love you too!"

"Thank you! Thank you! Very very very very much." Rahul again drew her closely to him.

How had nearly two hours managed to fly by? A couple of people had started toward the road by the field. There was the occasional sound of a bicycle bell. Someone was taking their water buffalo out for the day. Now the worry was that goat herders might come to this spot for the shrubs.

Anjali's clothes were soiled with leaves and grass. Rahul's were in the same state. They both stood up.

"It's not a good idea for both of us to leave here at the same time. Someone will see us. I'll leave first and go back to my room," Rahul said.

Just then, Anjali said, "Rahul, there's something I wanted to tell you."

"What is it?"

"Last night Lacchu Guru, that goonda, he came over and was drinking with my brother and was talking about you, Kartikeya, O.P., Parvez, and Pratap, all by name. The police just let him go. Papa phoned the police superintendent from Bhopal. I have the feeling that he may have talked with VC Agnihotri and will frame all of you in some police case. Be careful!"

Rahul was dumbfounded. Lacchu Guru and his accomplices had been turned over to the police by a crowd of three hundred students in the presence of the vice-chancellor. Dinamani had positively identified Lacchu Guru as the individual who had robbed, beaten, and acted savagely toward Sapam Tomba. Had VC Agnihotri and the police just been putting on an act that night?

This was beginning to seem like something right out of some formulaic Bombay action film. So this was the reality after all? Did Bollywood commercial cinema represent the most authentic and credible expression of the reality of our day and age, where everything is considered cheap, obscene, two-bit?

The intense spray of water from the shower completely refreshed Rahul. It was as if water from a clear, cool, mountain spring were cascading over his body.

Even his body was no longer its former self. It seemed that the cool, fresh September breeze was flowing through every fiber in his being, which shuddered with rapture.

Rahul realized that for the first time in his life he'd had an experience and a happiness that he could utterly call his own. Private, personal, and secret. A kind of treasure chest, hidden from all the others, carefully kept in some secure corner of his memory. Forever.

Now the heart sings with all its thousand voices
To hear this city of cells, my body, sing!

TWENTY-FOUR

The look of the Hindi department today was utterly different. It was as if a sick, old-fashioned Brahmin, dressed in dirty rags, the kind who carries out holy rituals in Haridwar or Allahabad, had just returned from a spa, suddenly cured, now a brand-new man, after enjoying a steambath, facial, color treatment, and full cosmetic makeover. Now he's wearing a snazzy checkered shirt: a smiling old swami.

Or it was like the rich old count from Tolstoy's story who preens himself before departing for the grand evening fête, affixing the special spring-loaded wig to keep his drooping face lifted up, and, arriving at the party, flirts with the beautiful, wily, and available young women who burn with the lust of unbridled social ambition.

So—today the Hindi department had been decorated. Plants and flowers had been placed everywhere. In addition to the decorative plastic plants, the botany department had provided marigolds, hazaaraa, gurahal, dahlias, kaner and other seasonal, scentless Western flowers brought from their gardens and crammed together with the rest. The girls had been given the tasks of threading the flower garlands for the guests and serving them the little plates of snacks.

When Rahul arrived at the department with Shaligaram and

Shailendra George, Anjali was with the other girls of the department. She was busy making garlands of white jasmine. She gave Rahul a quick look that concealed a smile.

The common room of the department had been emptied of furniture and transformed into an auditorium. Four chairs sat atop a white cloth, which had been spread over four low platforms pushed side by side. The chairs had been brought from the room of the chairman of the department, S. N. Mishra. They were big, with vinyl and foam cushions. In front of them were three tables covered by a white cloth, on top of which rested a huge bouquet of flowers. A shiny yellow silk banner hung on the wall behind displaying lovely red Devanagari lettering that read: "In Homor of Acharya Tribhuvan Narayan Mishra." The "n" in "honor" had become an "m," and it was shocking that no one had noticed. Rahul thought to himself that Hindi teachers can't even proofread.

Shailendra George informed him that of the four seats, the first one was reserved for Vice-Chancellor Ashok Kumar Agnihotri, the third one was for Head of Department S. N. Mishra, the last one to the left was for Padmashree Dr. Rajendra Tiwari, and on the second from the right, in between the vice-chancellor and the head of department, would be seated the former senior professor at Banaras Hindu University, Tribhuvan Narayan Mishra. He was an eminent scholar of mannerist Hindi poetry and had compiled a volume of the so-called best verses of Bihari's *Satsai*. He was a powerful strategist who maneuvered behind the scenes, influencing every countrywide university post in Hindi or editorial post in Hindi newspapers. Omnipresent member of every interview committee. Consultant to hundreds of Hindi foundations.

Department chair S. N. Mishra and Dr. Loknath Tripathi had left for the train station to receive Acharya Tribhuvan Narayan Mishra in the vice-chancellor's black, air-conditioned Ambassador car. Following behind were some senior students and some pet pupils.

A few minutes later the Marutis, Santros, Zens, and Maitzes began pulling up in front of the department. Hindi professors, readers, and lecturers came out of the cars. The down payments for the vehicles had been made with university funds, and the cars were bought on low-interest, easy-payment loans. These instructors, who make 25,000 to 30,000 rupees per month and hardly teach three or four months per year, now drove around in automobiles. They played the stock market. Their children were abroad to settle down. They strategically took trips and constantly went on strike for increased wages and expense allowances. Regardless of their different intellectual or political slants, the instructors had one common goal—rupees and promotion. All higher thinking and all academic priorities were subsumed by this one point.

There were exceptions to this, and the faces of these creatures had taken on distinct characteristics. They were like a handful of grains that had survived, accidentally, amid a vast pile of chaff of dead ideas and ideals. They were neglected in all possible ways. Buried under that towering mountain of chaff were the leftover seeds of some vanishing academic species. Sometime in the future an archaeologist would study these fossilized grains to determine which century and which decade they dated from.

More than a dozen professors and instructors stood in the hallway, spilling out of the Hindi department, waiting for the black

Ambassador to arrive. Classes had been rescheduled. The eighteen first-year MA students and the sixteen final-years all stood together. The three departmental underlings ran back and forth.

Sixteen teachers. Thirty-four students, ten of them female. And three underlings. This made a total of fifty-three human resources. Only three of the thirty-four students were non-Brahmin: Rahul, Shailendra George, and Shaligaram. Of the three underlings, one was a Yadav. Of the sixteen teachers, twelve were Brahmins, two were Baniyas, one Kayastha, and one Rajput. This was the demography of the Hindi department, the composition of its population.

Finally, at eleven thirty-two, the VC's black Ambassador pulled up to the steps of the department. In the back seat was the chair of the department, S. N. Mishra, sitting next to Acharya Tribhuvan Narayan. In the front seat next to the driver, Guddan Dubey, was Dr. Loknath Tripathi, looking content. Guddan Dubey was VC Agnihotri's nephew. A fake driver's license was procured for Guddan before giving him a permanent job as driver.

Guddan sprang out of the car and opened the back door. Loknath Tripathi emerged with a toothy smile. The professors and instructors standing in wait flashed their teeth in return. The commotion and clamor began. The department chair came around from the other side, folded his hands in supplication, and exhibited a very weak smile. Rahul made a mental note that Drs. Srivastav and Singh managed only half smiles, and that with great effort. It was clearly like pulling teeth for them.

Acharya Tribhuvan Narayan Mishra was seated in the car near the stairs leading up to the department. Then the back door of the Ambassador opened. Out came the former academic from Banaras Hindu University, eminent mannerist Hindi scholar, and current professor emeritus, Acharya Mishra, now ready to scale the steps of the Hindi department.

That's when the scene took shape.

First one real, worldly human foot emerged out of the open door of the black Ambassador, then another. He wore a white dhoti made of homespun and matching black natural-fiber sandals. His fingers were spread. He had dark, shiny legs. Greasy, as if he'd been rubbing them with ghee. As soon as those feet touched the ground, the uneasy, half-closed eyes on Dr. Loknath Tripathi's round, pudgy face gave the signal. It was as if his eyebrows danced for a moment on his forehead.

Padmashree Dr. Rajendra Tiwari was the first to reverentially touch the esteemed feet. After him, it was Dr. Shukla's turn, followed by Jha sahib, Pandey-ji, and Dr. Pant. Dr. Vajpeyi polished those dark hooves with his excited forehead. Dr. Aggrawal scoured the feet with his nose and cheeks. Dr. Dangwal combed his hair with those holy toes. Then came the turn of the students, who put on a surrealistic scene.

At the turn of the twenty-first century, this was an extremely authentic and original postmodern view of Hindi literature.

Rahul, Shailendra George, and Shaligaram stood off to one side, at a distance from this sacred ritual, as if they were sweepers or untouchables. Dogs and the fallen were prohibited from the ceremonial site by precepts of holy writ.

As the flabby, squat body of Acharya Tribhuvan Narayan

Mishra began ascending the stairs, adorned with a light yellow kosa-silk kurta, his shoulder draped with a white, neatly folded, starched angocha sprinkled with arrowroot, first-year MA student Vijay Pachauri Anand, beside himself, began to dance rapturously like Mirabai. "Hooray for our Derrida! Hooray for our Derrida!

"Hooray for our Bow-dree-la! Hooray for our Misra!

"Hooray for our Misra! Hooray for our Misra!"

It was difficult to say whether Pachauri was in fact singing like some ecstatic Baul, but when Rahul asked Shailendra George, "Did you hear that?" Shailendra George and Shaligaram answered in unison, "Sure, we caught something. It might have been Pachauri singing."

"Just watch! He'll get a faculty appointment very soon. Mark my words!" Who was it who'd said that?

Rahul sat in the very last row. The singing of the welcome song and the flower garlanding had concluded. Padmashree Tiwari gave the introduction for the acharya. There was a dire need for the department chair's speech to be translated into Hindi from whatever language he was speaking. He used countless words like *clerihew, zenzizenzizenzic, eleemosynary, sferics, wrixle, infundibulum, haruspex, etaoin shrdlu, wrele, therianthrope, bathykolpian, mithridate,* and *xenization.* In the middle of the introduction he stopped to recite something that sounded like a mantra. When at the end of the speech he declared, "It is through the grace and blessing of our eternal creator that the most highly esteemed Acharya Tribhuvan Narayan Mishra has today awoken each and every fiber of our bodies with feelings of joyful ecstasy by virtue of the intercourse he is having with us," some of the boys in the audience could barely suppress their laughter.

Acharya Tribhuvan Mishra recited what amounted to a tome detailing his participation in the World Hindi Conference in London, the Kabir Centenary Celebration in Germany, and, in New York, the Hindi conference to welcome the prime minister. Then he mentioned the new treatise on Kabir he was writing, according to which Kabir had renounced Islam and become a Brahmin. He offered his crystal-clear proof: Kabir was opposed to conversion and circumcision. In support of this supposition he recited one line of a Kabir poem and gave his interpretation of it: "Therefore he lived Hindu."

VC Agnihotri gave the closing remarks. He was overwhelmed by the acharya's erudition. He implored the acharya to convey his request to the central minister for Human Resources that practical subjects like journalism, media, internet, translation, etc. be added to the curriculum of the Hindi department. The acharya stood up right in the middle of Agnihotri's speech, asked to have the university budget prepared immediately and, amid the thundering applause, gave his assurance he could secure its approval in under a month.

. . . Sure, they'll teach those subjects here. Medieval gorilla, parasitical Pandey, and purohit. They'll start a website dedicated to horoscopes, palmistry, wizardry, and astrology. Hindi journalism will become a medium of hocus-pocus, fire ritual, and mantra chanting, and a place to learn how to become a clever ass-kisser to the powers that be. And translation will be nothing more than to Sanskritize English words . . .

What a bind. On the one side the Western powers, on the other side Brahmin pandits. Is freedom of language any less of a question than political freedom? Rahul thought. "Western power and Brahmin pandits are just two sides of the same coin!"

"What!? Did you say something, Rahul?" Shailandra George said, taken aback.

"No, I was just wondering if the samosas and gulab jamun were ever going to make their way over here," Rahul answered.

His eyes continuously scanned the crowd for Anjali. She was sitting somewhere in the front row. Rahul noticed that Abha, Anima, Renu, and Seema had entered the room during the acharya's speech. Anjali was the daughter of a state minister, after all. If she hadn't been sitting in the front would she really come to the back row where he was? Feelings of simultaneous want and defeat closed in on Rahul. Just then the underling Kailash Yadav thrust a paper plate in front of Rahul's face. The warm smell of hot samosas rushed into Rahul's nose. In the front rows, the snacks were being served by Sharmistha, Lata, and Chandra.

As people milled about in front of the department building, and the VC and the acharya readied themselves to set off for the guesthouse in the black Ambassador, a Tata Safari pulled up. A six-foot-tall, white-kurta-pajama-clad, smiling, mustachioed man got out. Behind him were three more dressed in pants and shirts. The smiling moustache man had a cell phone in one hand and a bouquet of flowers in the other. He came forward, touched the feet of the acharya, and gave him the bouquet. Then he shook the hand of the VC.

"That's Lakhan Lal Pandey, aka Lakkhu Bhaiya," Shaligaram whispered into Rahul's ear. "Head of the town council."

Then Shailendra squeezed Rahul's hand. "That's Lacchu Guru, aka Lakshpati Lal Pandey's older brother."

Rahul was stunned.

Right then S. N. Mishra and Dr. Loknath Tripathi glanced at the three boys whispering among themselves. Balram Pandey's eagle eye was also trained on them.

Something like a frightening little black moth rested like a moustache below his nose, below those eyes.

Rahul, Shailendra, and Shaligaram all shuddered.

As Rahul lay in his bed in Room 252 that night, he said to O.P., "Today I saw those eyes. I'm really scared, yaar."

"What are you talking about? Are you having a dream?" O.P. switched off the light in the room. Now in the darkness, those two eyes looked down on him right above his head.

"Those eyes were so terrifying, O.P.! They were just like the Führer's." In the dark, Rahul said, "it's not a dream, it's real." His voice was shaking. "They're still right here, in this room. Above my head."

"You just seem scared, Rahul. Quiet down and go to sleep. We'll talk in the morning." O.P. rolled over.

Rahul couldn't sleep that night.

This was no insomnia, but rather the kind of fear that Jews the world over must have felt during the 1930s and '40s. So, are they going to send people like me to the gas chamber now? Because, by chance, I have no ill will toward Shailendra George, Masood, and Shaligaram? Because I'm religious, a believer? Because I dearly love the splendor and variety of this country, and the fundamental promises inscribed in the constitution?

A film loop kept repeating in Rahul's head, causing him deep anxiety. In this loop, all the faces—of VC Agnihotri, Department Head S. N. Mishra, the acharya, Dr. Loknath Tripathi, hostel warden Chandramani Upadhyay, Radharaman Chaturvedi, Dr. Dangwal, Dr. Pant, and Dr. Joshi—were jumbled together. As soon as the VC's face came into focus, the face of Padmashree Tiwari would be superimposed. Earlier the coal-black caste-marked face of the acharya had appeared clearly, but as it rose to the surface, out came the familiar face of the prime minister. Suddenly, a cloud of smoke, and there was the fat, licentious Nikhlani, relaxing in the luxury cabin in a yacht or sprawled out in an island resort getting massaged by a team of Miss Third Worlds and fashion models from rich European countries, washing down pill after pill of Viagra with expensive scotch, immersed in unending pleasure and a boundless feast, and speaking into his cell phone, "Hello . . . Hello! Get me to the PM! Nikhlani here! Sell, sell, sell! Everything must go! We're buying everything. Privatize the Indian government, pandit! Privatize defense! The police, the army, the paramilitaries, we'll buy 'em all, pandit! If someone gets in the way, shoot the motherfucker. They're Naxalites, they're Pakistani ISI agents! I've got high blood pressure. Pandit, be quick, hurry up, hurry up!"

Rahul thought he heard the sound of a jeep pulling up outside, followed by the sound of footsteps.

Now comes the knock on the door. Lacchu Guru will be there with his pistol. Not a pistol, an AK-47. Even the six-foot-three-inch ostrich will be killed along with Rahul. His own corpse will lie where Sapam's lies, and where Chaitanya's broken dholak and little cymbals lie. Beside the bespectacled eyes of Gandhi-ji.

It was a dark, frightening tunnel with no sleep inside. It was airless, filled with only fear and danger. It was suffocating. Dear god! How I wish that yellow butterfly would come and keep me safe under its wing.

You are my power and strength, Anjali. *I love you really.* Save me, please. However you can.

Rahul couldn't remember when sleep came to him that night, if at all. When his eyes opened, the golden rays of sunrise were falling on his burning forehead. The morning sunlight and Rahul's head both burned inside with some kind of fire.

"I have no clue what you were muttering about last night," O.P. said. "Why are your eyes red? You're not getting a fever, are you? What's *happened* to you?" O.P. placed his hand on Rahul's forehead.

Rahul closed his eyes. There was Anjali. Her eyes looked worried. Distressed. Anxious. She covered Rahul with her yellow parasol.

"You're such a good friend, O.P.!" Rahul said. A tear fell from the corner of his eye onto the pillow.

O.P. went to the dispensary to get some paracetamol—there had been a recent rash of viral and dengue fever.

TWENTY-FIVE

It was a five-day bone-shattering fever. Yet Rahul still stood in front of the window gazing toward the field below. The bobbing yellow spot, the little butterfly fluttering up from the valley toward the university—Rahul didn't see either during those five days, not once.

"Dehydration's the real danger. Drink lots of water. With sugar and salt," said Govind Nema, who lived in C. V. Raman Hostel and was doing research in pharmacology.

Pratap, Ataluri, Niketan, Kartikeya, Madhusudan, Parvez, Praveen, Masood—everyone came regularly to visit Rahul in his room. They'd play cards. Sing a few songs. Smoke beedis and cigarettes. They even held a meeting of the SMTF.

Shaligaram and Shailendra George from the Hindi department both came. Rana, Manmohan, and Raju too. Rahul was feeling so distressed he asked everyone about Anjali. How was she doing? What was she doing? Has she said anything? Why hasn't he been seeing her from his window?

On the third day, Hemant Barua arrived, smiling, and placed Rahul's hand around a little slip of paper. "*Message from your bird. She gave this to me on my way to the department.*"

The little slip of paper was light green, and in a scrawling, childlike handwriting was written in blue, "Get Well Soon." And below, in blue letters, was her signature, A-N-J-I, "Anji."

Hemant had learned that for the past few days Anjali had been coming to campus by car, with a driver. She was a bit distraught. Then Hemant added, laughing, "But don't lose your head, Rahul. I happen to know she really loves you. From now on, I'm putting the two of you in a joint de facto file, which will be updated daily."

So much sweat was pouring out of Rahul's body that he had to constantly wipe himself off with a towel.

"See! I told you the kind of paracetamol that would really cure this bastard," O.P. said. "I ran over to the dispensary for no reason. Now that he's got his love note, his fever will go away."

"Oh, so it's not dengue!" Hemant exclaimed. "It's that Nana Patekar disease."

"Not malaria, but 'love-aria,'" the six-foot ostrich wailed.

"Shut up," Rahul said, and started to cough.

Yet this period of time wasn't so bright and happy. It wasn't simply that drops of dew were falling on its leaves; the leaves were also being ravaged by fire and ice.

Two of the three students Rahul had been tutoring stopped coming. He found out someone told one of his students, the sales tax officer Jaiswal's daughter, that he was an indecent character. Someone had informed M. L. Gupta, of Gupta Transport and Travel, that Rahul had once been caught in the act of teaching the Kama Sutra to a girl and, after a good beating, was run out of town. He would have lost his third tutee had Pratap not rescued him by saying something to his uncle, a policeman.

It all added up to this: the critters were on the move. They were the proprietors of the biggest rumor and falsehood factory in the history of India. If they wished to eradicate any individual or group, first they'd unite and, once together, they'd erect a heap of rumor and lies. The apprenticeship, passed through the centuries from generation to generation, came in very handy. Brahminical texts and all of the puranas lent proof to the lies. Just a few years back the Babri Masjid incident in Ayodhya gave all Hindi newspapers occasion to support the lies. VC Agnihotri, the students learned, had indicated at a meeting of the university's governing body that he'd recently come into possession of information that certain Communists and Naxalites living in the hostels were fanning flames among the other students. The names of Kartikeya Kajle and Madhusudan were mentioned, both of whom had spotless academic records, and it was suggested they had criminal records in Maharashtra and Kerala.

Dr. Dangwal and Dr. Loknath Tripathi took the girls to the side and warned them, "Keep your distance from Rahul. He's an indecent character."

Rahul's head was spinning. Why was this happening to him? Because he was a hardworking student? Because he didn't kiss up to any of the teachers? Because he and the other members of the SMTF got together and stopped the goondas from robbing, beating, and acting savagely toward students who'd come from different regions, different states? Was it because he had the kind of body and face that could not be made corrupt?

Or was it because he was of indeterminate lineage, but not a Brahmin, who, by accident, crawled into the medieval cave of Hindi literature while pursing a girl? Or was he some African slave who'd arrived in the middle of a Roman city? Or an outcaste with a gong tied around his neck so he can sound the alarm on his own, and give warning: "Please, kind Brahmin sir, keep your distance, as a vile untouchable is now passing! Kindly save yourself from contaminating your lordship's self and have the good grace to avoid contact with the shadow of this base creature! Come, see how some Shabuk-like untouchable is again doing penance in your glorious Vedic language, and off with his head! At the hands of a Kshatriya. Then cut up the severed head with Parashuram's blade. Throw his wife into the fire, kidnap her, and if that still hasn't done the trick, call her a whore, a loose woman, and banish her from town.

"But keep in mind that this time, somewhere beyond the city limits of your capital, she'll find refuge in a little hut inhabited by an outcaste. And this time too, that very outcaste, who you'll call a bandit, will write another enduring epic poem.

"And now, dear bastards, once again I give you—the great poet Valmiki!"

Woo whee! Woo whee!

At eleven o'clock at night there was an uproar in the hostel. O.P. came rushing in with the news that Niketan and Masood had gone to see the film *Satya* at the Ganesh Talkies, where Lacchu Guru and his lackeys caught sight of them. They goondas surrounded the two boys and beat them senseless. They drew blood from Masood's left eye and fractured a rib, his right wrist, and left thumb. Niketan had also been injured.

In next morning's edition of *Janvani* on page three, which promised "All India" but gave only local news, ran the headline,

"Lust-Crazed Hostel Student Beaten for Harassing Girl." According to the story, a male member of a certain minority community was physically harassing a girl of a certain other community in front of the Ganesh Talkies when an agitated crowd formed and beat the living daylights out of him and his associate. Police officer in charge Vijay Narayan Sharma told *Janvani* that charges have been filed against the two students.

According to the de facto file at the Max Cyber Cafe, the publisher of *Janvani* was a regularly attending darbari at VC Agnihotri's court. Monthly installments were paid to conceal news about corruption and chicanery connected with the university. Puff pieces on VC Agnihotri were continually printed in the newspaper along with regular reports commending his activities. Most evenings the publisher could be seen with VC Agnihotri, drinking whiskey and burping loudly in curtained cabin no. 2 in the family section of the only bar in town, the Asiana. He was that breed of animal who in political terms is a "socialist" and in cultural terms a "fascist." In other words, a true Brahminist.

Hemant Barua and Kartikeya were sharing a joke. Hemant said, "I've changed the spelling of 'globalization' by changing the 'b' to a 'c.'"

"What do you mean?" asked O.P.

"Here we don't have 'globalization' but rather 'glocalization.' In other words 'g' plus *localization*." It wasn't clear from Hemant's tone of voice if he was angry or being sarcastic.

"Tell us, Hindi literature recruit, how do you translate that into Hindi?" Kartikeya Kajle asked Rahul. He was from Pune and his mother tongue was Marathi.

"Well, the 'g' gives us 'grisly,' and localization stays the same, so, 'grisly localization,'" Rahul said in a weary voice.

"That's the true reality," said Kartikeya.

The reality was also that the centuries-old factory of falsehood and rumors had begun clanging and banging away, ready to take on Rahul and the others, whose only crime was to be neither immoral nor corrupt. That and—in this age of profiteers, conmen, and vice—they were poor, their pockets were empty, and they were guided by conscience.

TWENTY-SIX

Shaligaram and Shailendra came with news that neither O.P. nor Rahul could believe. But once the six-foot-three skeleton accepted that the information was true, he did a dance worthy of Michael Jackson and ran off as fast as the queen of Indian track and field, P. T. Usha, to inform the others.

What happened was this: that day, each class from every department elected their counselors to the student union. Balram Pandey stood as a candidate for the first-year students of the Hindi department. Everyone knew he was the hopeful of Dr. Loknath Tripathi, since Balram even cooked for the professor at his home. Vijay Pachauri had nominated Balram, and Ram Narayan Chaturvedi had seconded the motion. It seemed as if he'd win, unopposed.

Shailendra George continued the story with a smile on his face. "So I just stood up and nominated Rahul for the fun of it. I thought even if he only gets two votes, Pandey shouldn't be handed the election unopposed. Shaligaram was just about to stand up to second the nomination, when . . ."

"Anjali Joshi," Shaligaram cut in excitedly, "stood up from the girls' side and said, 'I second Rahul's name.'"

"We did a quick count and figured if all the girls voted for our side, that would still leave Rahul with only eight votes, compared to Balram Pandey's nine Brahmin votes, which would cinch it for him," Shailendra said.

"We readied ourselves for defeat. But when the counting was done, Rahul had gotten nine votes and Balram Pandey, eight. He lost by one vote," Shaligaram said, clapping his hands. "Someone defected from their side."

"And I know who it was!" Shailendra George declared as if he were a spy. "It was Sudip Pant. Sharmistha brought him over to our side. Those two have a thing going on."

O.P. had returned with the others. He'd brought a pound of roasted peanuts. They extracted Balbir from the mess hall and ordered ten cups of pauper's chai.

It was with roasted peanuts and chai that the unexpected election victory was celebrated.

Ten days had passed. During his fever, Rahul had sped through Hazariprasad Dwivedi's novel *Anamdas ka Potha*, enjoying it tremendously. After the news from Shaligaram and Shailendra about his election as councillor, Rahul stayed awake long after O.P. had gone to sleep.

The novel tells the story of a celibate monk, dwelling in a hut in the forest, who sees a woman for the first time in his life and experiences a sweet shiver up his spine, impossible to articulate. That night, Rahul experienced the same sweet, unexplainable shiver time and again. All over his body, and all over his soul— everywhere Anjali had touched.

"Why did you second my name? Why, Anji?" he whispered that night, all alone, like a bird might. Crouching in a nest hanging from a branch, suddenly stung by a blast of wind at night, the bird might mutter to itself, to the wind, or to the branch.

That night, Rahul had forgotten how his life, and the lives of countless others like him, was like a boat with weak sails, trapped inside a typhoon, in a decisive battle for its very existence, struggling desperately against the deranged and omnivorous waves churned up by the violent and crazed ocean of today's world. Each time, the imperative of the waves wagered with their lives, his and the others'. And each time their lives were spared, by chance, by some unexpected miracle.

That night Rahul felt he was sleeping safe and sound on deck of some ship, as if he'd just been saved by the skin of his teeth from a Titanic-like disaster, and was now on a carefree cruise in calm and peaceful waters, sailing on an imponderable, loving ocean. A full autumn moon was in the sky, really nothing more than Anjali's presence. She was silently composing a new life story, written on his forehead with her moonbeams.

Just at the point of falling into a deep sleep, Rahul remembered part of a poem of his beloved poet Lorca:

On my forehead
The moon's immortality
I want to sleep for a short time
An hour, a night, a week, a year
A century, perhaps
I am tired, endlessly tired

TWENTY-SEVEN

O.P. grabbed Rahul by the collar from behind. Rahul had seen the yellow butterfly through the window, fluttering up from the valley below, had thrown on his pants and a T-shirt in a hurry, and was dashing out the door. "Do you really believe I think you're going 'jogging' so early in the morning? Am I that stupid?"

"So where *am* I going, then?" Rahul asked like a good boy.

O.P. landed his fist on Rahul's back. "Go, go to your paracetamol. But just remember that one of these days, it'll be me who saves your behind. Now get outta here!"

Rahul leapt down the stairs three at a time. The fever had sapped his energy—who knows where all this energy and enthusiasm had come from.

You are my power Anji, my shakti!

But as soon as he saw her, he knew something was wrong. She was looking all around and said, "Don't come running like that, Rahul! *Things have changed now.* Let's go over there, quick!"

They came to the area behind the storeroom, a safe little corner surrounded by two big rocks and lentinas. Anjali closed the parasol and hid it under a bush. She needed to get something off her chest in one big breath. Rahul saw the worry in her face. She took hold of Rahul's arm as if she were holding onto a thing about to get away, as if she were a boatman making one last attempt to seize his oar being swept away by a strong current. Rahul trembled, she held his arm with such force!

Tears filled Anjali's eyes. "Everything's okay for now, but we have to stay alert," she said.

"What happened? Tell me," Rahul said, smoothing back the hair that had fallen in her face.

"Someone said something to my brother about us. And some crazy things were said about you, like you take drugs, like you're a questionable character, like you're a Naxalite."

Rahul was shaking. "Who said all of this?"

"They also said that before coming here you were mixed up in some criminal case and expelled from another university . . ."

"Bastards!" Rahul's blood was boiling. "Everything's a lie."

"You think I don't know that, Rahul?" Anjali said, taking his hand in her lap. "Anyone who knows you believes you, Rahul," she continued. "But how many people know you? And if they don't know you, they'll believe whatever they hear. Right? That's why lies are always more potent."

"Jesus!" Rahul was in agony. "Kartikeya'd said that they'd started operations at their factory."

"Factory?" Anjali didn't understand.

"Never mind," Rahul said. "Tell me what *you* think about me."

"What *I* think about you?" Anjali said as if he'd set off a storm. She looked at him with knowing eyes. By the time Rahul could move his face into position, she'd already pounced. "This is what I think! And this! And . . . and . . ."

In an abandoned place between two walls of rock, a synchronized ecstasy, a madness, welled up with equal force inside the two bodies, spilling over until they were crashing together, flying together.

Their faces were wet and sticky. Their clothing had gotten wrinkled, covered in little dried blades of grass and leaves.

"The girls have really supported me. Sharmishtha, Lata, Chandra. Anima, Abha, and Neera Didi, from your anthropology department, all of them came to visit me at home," Anjali said, taking a deep breath. "While you were having a grand old time enjoying your fever."

"I kept looking out the window for you. Why did you start coming to campus by car?"

"What could I have done? My brother got a driver so he could spy on me." Then Anjali smiled. "But now everything's okay. All we have to do is be a little careful."

"But who's behind all of this?" Rahul asked.

"All of them. All the Brahmins," Anjali said. She thought silently, then added, as if scolding, "But don't forget, Rahul, you won the election because of Brahmins, and they saved your skin this time, too."

That startled Rahul. What confusion! He thought for a moment. Then he pulled her toward him.

So, her too! Dear god, what does all this mean?

Kinnu Da once said, "In the history of this country no caste has ever maintained a fixed position. In one area they're high on the ladder. In another, lower. In some other field, they're in the middle. *These castes have fascinating mobility, downward and upward.* The caste that has risen to the top of any field, in any place, is simply the one that's seized power. These castes are capable of exceptional dynamism! That's why they're not so fanatical, or orthodox, since more dynamism and more variety equals greater liberality and greater openness.

"But there is one group that has carved out a static place for itself. Totally immovable. Right at the top. For thousands of years. This is the Brahmin caste. Free from physical labor. Illustrious representatives of a culture reaping pleasure from others' work, struggle, and sacrifice. With its leave from labor, this caste created a kingdom of heaven it inhabited for centuries; during this time, it gave birth to another kingdom, one of illusion, and filled it with language, superstition, schemes, codes of law, false consciousness —all of which it used to control the lives and minds of those from other castes, and to rule all of society.

"Rahul, you must have read the Israeli poet Amichai, 'A Very Active Head on a Very Pensive Trunk.' A cunning, conspiracy-filled, racing head on top of a good-for-nothing, vagrant body. The kind of head you could drive the straightest of nails into, and it would come out a screw or spring."

Kinnu Da turned serious and said, *"They are the greatest and deadliest power manipulators for centuries!* Nowhere in all of world history will you find a caste of clever magicians so bent on cinching power into the grip of their vise. *A well-organized nexus of power manipulators.* This group is capable of doing anything for power and money. And it's the great misfortune of this country that they've always been successful. Even today!"

Oh, so that's what it means! Chaos reigned in Rahul's mind. That's the reason the world of Hindi literature produced such lovely poetic odes for Queen Victoria. Songs were written to sing the glory of King George V upon his visit to India. Poems and articles were written during the Raj in praise of the British: you have saved us from untouchables, heretics, barbarians, and the butchers, also known as Muslims. During the Mughal Raj, they wrote couplets and quatrains and dactylic poems in Braj and Awadhi to flatter their rulers. Thank you, thank you a thousand times over for saving us from those insolent, wild, base, boorish villagers, and from the fallen castes.

Now at the turn of the twenty-first century, these everlasting upper casters of Hindi literature have started their sycophancy in flattery of corrupt bureaucrats and politicians. Rahul's soul was crisscrossed with shame, disgust, and dejection.

Am I working toward an MA in Hindi literature or Brahmin literature? In order to get across his revolutionary message, Buddha had to abandon Sanskrit, seeking refuge in Pali. So now, must Hindi be dropped in favor of using some other language to formulate ideas to provoke change? This means that now neither Buddha nor Gandhi would be a possibility in Hindi. Only Acharya Tribhuvan Narayan Mishra and the Padmashree Tiwari will survive!

"Oh, shit, shit, shit!" came out of Rahul's mouth.

Anjali was looking at him with bewilderment. "What happened? You seem a little frazzled."

"I'm okay," Rahul said, kissing her forehead. "*I love you too much!* I love you like I'm some kind of madman." He stopped for a moment and gazed at her with a look of anguish, nearly imperceptible. Anjali recognized it, and knew herself what it was. Rahul's face was now showing signs of swoon.

"Believe me, please! I really truly love you, Miss Joshi!" Rahul said in a weak voice.

"Tsk!" Anjali said, slapping Rahul's cheek. But the slap she had lovingly placed on Rahul's cheek at the "Miss Joshi" joke wasn't a joking matter. It was a matter of deep suffering.

From all sides at once a windstorm suddenly sprang up, gusts crashing and cutting into one another. Anjali grabbed her parasol and clutched it tightly. Luckily it wasn't open, otherwise it would have been carried away in the wind like all the dried leaves, grass, and plastic bags swirling in the air.

"We call this kind of storm a 'dammon' in my village—a 'demon' of wind. People say that if you chase down the first leaf blown in the storm and press it between your teeth, you'll disappear, become completely invisible. Then no one will be able to see you," Rahul said.

"I see!" Anjali said. "Should we try to find the first leaf?"

"We'll never find that leaf with all that trash flying around, and even if we did, how can one leaf make two people disappear?" Rahul said, his mood lightening.

"Of course two people can disappear!" Anjali countered.

"From one leaf?" Rahul asked, uncertain.

"Sure!" Anjali was smiling.

"How?" It was perplexing to Rahul.

"No, really, they can disappear. I said they could, didn't I? So what do you mean, 'how'?" Anjali said, pushing her point.

"But . . ." Rahul still wasn't getting the logistics. "How?"

"Like this!" Anjali said, and wrapped herself around Rahul with all her might. Rahul felt that the two of them really had disappeared. No one could see them now. But they could see everyone—the entire world, the whole town, from one end of the sky to the other.

At one end of the field, behind a makeshift storeroom, at the foot of the hill, in a secret, deserted place between two big gray walls of rock, Anjali and Rahul had become invisible. All that remained was Anjali's yellow parasol. That too was shut closed, hidden under a lentina bush.

And what about the other parasol? That was a butterfly, which had one day transformed its very form, playing a trick on the whole world. In front of everyone's eyes and in broad daylight.

TWENTY-EIGHT

"You've stopped going to the gym?" O.P. asked. "You've been looking really weak lately."

Rahul thought for a moment and said, "I'm still kind of afraid of something, but I don't know why. I don't think I did the right thing when I transferred to the Hindi department, yaar."

"I don't get it," Hemant Barua said with a laugh. "Nothing's ruined yet. *To hell with Hindi.* Take a short-term course at NIIT or Zap and get out of that hellhole."

"It's the same situation in the Urdu department," Parvez said. "If Hindi's a hellhole, then Urdu's the underworld. Shahid didn't even finish his first year. In the end, he gave up and opened a repair shop for fridges and TVs. Now he's saying he'll go to Dubai."

"I'm not going anywhere. I'll stay right in the thick of it, I'll fight right in the thick of it, and I'll be killed right in the thick of it," Rahul laughed. It wasn't a lighthearted laugh.

"Right, you dumb bastard, why pull yourself out of that gutter? That's where your paracetamol is, where your parasol is, where your butterfly is, where your bird is. Everything's in Hindi," the ostrich cried out, and started humming frighteningly out of tune, "*My living is here, and dying is here, so where else can I go?*"

"Cut it out!" Rahul screamed. Everyone laughed.

Rahul's thirst for Anjali increased each time they met. He felt as if the sea inside him began anxiously churning whenever he came close to Anjali, ready to swallow up the entire world with its cities, mountains, and people.

Each time he got back after seeing Anjali he felt as if a towering, mad wave born from his sea inside had crashed against the rocky base of a mountain, rebuffed, and now returning. Despairing, and in shock.

What remains, then, is the sea, each time left alone with its murky melancholy.

Today Anjali wore jeans and a loose white T-shirt. This time she and Rahul were on the third floor of the library in the corner of the south wall. There was a filthy, dusty window that had been shut tight for years and hardly let any sunlight through. Then, nothing but stacks and stacks of books.

In a narrow space between two book stacks, Anjali and Rahul conspired to disappear. The smell of old books, the faint light barely coming in through the window, the moisture from the damp walls, the fine dust . . . Rahul and Anjali locked themselves in an embrace with such force, filled with such longing, it was as if they needed the entire expanse of the earth to make their wish come true. The space between stacks of books was too narrow.

Never before had Rahul lifted Anjali up and she wrapped her legs around his waist. Those seconds were like suddenly finding oneself in the middle of a misty twilight. Both could scarcely catch their breath. Rahul's half-closed eyes opened from their trance and regarded Anjali's face, which had changed completely. Now it was some flower being burned by fire, quivering, wilting into an enchanting potion.

In that hazy moment, Anjali's eyes appeared to Rahul. What eyes they were, watching a dream unfold of another world. Her eyes were strictly focused, but what she was staring at was some scene far off in the distance, of another realm, another time. She looked as if she would swoon.

They were like two fish swimming in the strong current of a stream, having touched one another, yet their tiny bodies still full of such longing for one another that they continue to swim, and they still want to pierce one another through and through. Time and again their bodies make innocent, improbable gestures to extract themselves from each other's insides.

Rahul's hand moved toward the zipper of Anjali's jeans.

"No, no, what are you doing?" Anjali's words scattered into the darkness, a semiconscious objection.

"Please let me," Rahul's whisper trembled in the air.

"No, not here," Anjali pulled him tightly toward her.

"Where, then?" Rahul asked, his question floating heavenward.

Then a muted thud, as if a book had fallen off the shelf. Anjali and Rahul froze like statues and held their breath.

Padmashree Tiwari and Balram Pandey were looking for something, a book, on the shelf next to the main door.

Rahul gently eased Anjali back down. The two of them crouched down and hid beneath the shelf, trying to control their nervous breathing.

Rahul finally took a deep breath only after Padmashree Tiwari and Balram Pandey had left. Rahul noticed a book peering at them from the shelf behind: Ján Otcenásek's novel *Romeo, Juliet, and Darkness.*

Caught in the middle of Nazi soldiers' boot steps and gunfire, two innocent, helpless teenagers, a boy and a girl, hide inside a room for one full year. The two children grow up between the fear that death might come at any moment, and with their love for one another. Rahul had read this novel just the month before, in Nirmal Verma's beautiful Hindi translation that read like poetry.

In the corner, next to an ailing wall that could collapse at any moment on top of it, a very delicate plant grew slowly, but surely and lushly, like a riddle amid spreading violence and fear. Like a lifeline in the darkness of sin, in a daring attempt fraught by risk, this, the purest blossom and primary bloom waged struggle in a demonic time.

Rahul kissed Anjali's hand. "So tell me: when?" he asked. His voice sprang from the solitude and longing of that sea.

"Thursday," Anjali said as if she'd already had this day in mind from the beginning.

"Why does it have to be Thursday? That's seven days away. Why not tomorrow?" Rahul was perplexed.

"Crazy boy. That's the day there are only two classes," Anjali said.

"Right, Dr. Loknath Tripathi's Bhakti class and Rajendra Tiwari's class on Vidyapati," Rahul said. "You are brilliant."

Anjali straightened her clothing, took a brush from her purse, and fixed her hair.

"Wait. But where?" Rahul got worried.

"I have no idea," Anjali answered, and left.

Rahul stood for a long time in that narrow space between the bookshelves, absentmindedly taking books from the shelf and leafing through them.

Oddly enough Rahul didn't notice the damp, musty smell of the old books, but rather took in the fresh, sensuous fragrance of Anjali's body that still surrounded him.

Rahul remained for awhile, but just before leaving, he filled his lungs, inhaling the air slowly and deeply.

Lay me on the hills and mountains
of thirst
Burn me in the sun, and dance
dance in its flames
Dance as a fountain of water

Dissolve into ink and write me in the sky
O mirrors
There read of me, then grin at me
O mirrors
Before killing me
O mirrors
For I am your life

The meaning of these lines from Shamsher's poem slowly opened up to Rahul. Reading poetry and uncovering its meaning: this is the true living of life.

TWENTY-NINE

Time was passing, days were turning. The days were filled with contrasts never before seen in all of history.

The internationally known geologist Dr. Watson had resigned from the university and left for Australia. The evening before the day he left, Dr. Watson went out to gaze at the mountains for the last time. Kartikeya was a student in his department. He said, "Dr. Watson was very sad. He stood for a long time in front of the well where Sapam committed suicide. He pried out a troublesome rock from the crumbling platform of the well. It was an odd rock, almost translucent.

"He spent a long time standing there staring at the rock. Then there was a flash of lightning in his eyes. It was as if he'd gathered all his fury and he suddenly threw that rock into the well. I peered into the well. It wasn't that dark, and I could see Sapam's Liberty flip-flop still floating down there."

Dr. Watson had said, "That was a fossil. A fossil of a conch shell, thousands of years old. A conch from a time when this was a sea. You people use the same conch to perform your puja . . . a part of puja to Krishna."

Kartikeya said they'd asked Dr. Watson why he decided to leave.

Dr. Watson had laughed and replied, "Because I don't feel 'safe' here. Times have changed. Now I'm afraid."

"Me too, Kartikeya!" Rahul said in a weak voice.

"Who's not afraid? Is *anyone* safe here?" Kartikeya scolded. "All of the vile, dangerous, base, and hedonistic things we've imported from the West. Gambling, profiteering, weapons, fizzy, toxic drinks, alcohol, pornography, pizza, cars. People here have lost their minds pursuing this merchandise of thrill, titillation, frenzy, and violence. People here want the worst from the West, but want to kill and destroy the best it has to offer. These are its assassins. Enemies."

Kartikeya's eyes had become red with rage. "Buy a gun from America. Use it to shoot Jesus. Use the vilest thing invented by the West to commit the greatest murder in history. Buy a car from Japan. Use it to run over Buddha's head. Find biochemical weapons from Iraq. Use them to kill the Prophet Mohammad. Get a missile launcher from Israel. Use it to blow Jehovah's body to bits. Devil barbarians!" Kartikeya was out of breath.

"But really, what can we do?" Someone uttered this sentence, and it floated down, lodged itself inside everyone sitting in the room, and twitched like the wounded tail of a gecko.

Kartikeya's words echoed in Rahul's head. "They'll take the fire from the Rig Veda and use it to burn all the Vedas. They'll take the trishul trident from the Puranas and use it to impale Shiva and Vishnu. They'll get their hands on a Bramastra and launch it to annihilate all of creation."

They will throw all enlightened souls in the history of mankind into conflict with one another, then crush them underfoot.

They are the Critters, sent here by Satan from some other world.

They are Ravana's offspring, returned by the sea, who now hold everything in their hands: power, capital, language, words, newspapers, computers, television, satellites launched into outer space, atomic bombs, and quite a huge market.

"What kind of realization was this?" Rahul wondered.

He felt like sending an email to the president of the United States that would read, "If you truly consider yourself a follower of Jesus, then remove yourself from these all-powerful salesmen. They are the ones who murdered the compassion of Christ."

THIRTY

Things were changing fast. A store selling seized customs goods opened next to Max Cyber Cafe. Pepsi, Coke, and Miranda stalls were springing up everywhere. So were fast-food joints, and in one of them the waiters even wore Nawab-style plumed turbans and creased uniforms. There, the same burger you could get in a regular dhaba or snack van for 5 rupees would cost you 20. The dosa that normally cost 12 would cost 22 rupees. What was surprising was that this kind of shop was most prevalent. Noodles, pizza, fried chicken, ice cream, burgers, Manchurian—a whole new menu of things to eat and drink had arrived. A big store selling greeting cards, cake, and gift items had opened next to the university's supermarket. There were four shops on campus selling paan and cigarettes. One was right in front of the hostel, and under the guise of selling Ayurvedic medicine sold everything from "honey raisin" bhang balls to the same thing in a form you can inhale: ganja and hashish, brown sugar, and white powder. Condoms (both domestic and foreign brands) and oral contraception were now completely out in the open. Everywhere were AIDS posters and slogans, and advertisements for ultrasound and abortion.

At night, everything from the hard stuff (Boney Scott, Macdowell, Old Monk, Diplomat, Director's Special) to the cheap stuff (bathtub mahua sold in plastic pouches) to the rough stuff (liquor made from a herb said to revive the dead) was sold at the fruit juice stand behind the post office. The police took their weekly cut, and that was that.

Numbers games and the lottery made for big business everywhere. There were three local cable channels that showed porn late at night—"blue films." During the day the same stations basically showed sermons of Asaram Bapu, Murari Bapu, and others like them. As religious programming proliferated—the bhajans, the revivals, the preaching—so increased crime, rape, abortion, murder, thuggery, and theft. Commerce in women, and violence against them, increased in proportion to the number of beauty pageants and fashion shows.

Temples were springing up everywhere. It was a way to "clean" illegally seized land and black market cash. Untold amounts of money were circulating among just a few people. Some 45 of every 100 rupees in the country was undeclared, illegal, black. Every day new businesses were set up that existed only on paper, only to disappear in the middle of the night along with people's money. Fake companies were openly exchanged on the stock market, defrauding honest citizens of their life savings. Farmers, unemployed youth, conned women, all were committing suicide. NGOs and private schools were sprouting like mushrooms and making a killing.

Apparently, twenty women from the girls' hostel frequented the Asiana bar and the new three-star hotel, Naurang, and worked as call girls. Everyone knew who they were, but kept quiet. The girls' connections went right to the top. Cars came and went from the girls' hostel. These were the "empowered" women. A certain brand of feminism had taken over, dictating that a hardworking

girl could become a nurse, teacher, stenographer, typist, or a working "lady" who also attends to household chores. Or, she could
become a "read the Gita, become a Sita" kind of overworked,
downtrodden yet pious wife. But if she becomes a sex worker, in
no time at all she'll have that nice house and start riding around in
cars.

What sort of paradox was this? No one objected if a woman
sold herself in the market. But it was verboten for her to want to
establish a human, private connection with someone.

If Anjali were to win the crown of Miss Femina India, the
personal prestige of PWD Minister L. K. Joshi would only in-
crease. But if Anjali cultivates a human, emotional, and real relationship with me, she'll get nothing but notoriety, Rahul thought.

This is the way the market doled out its funds. This was how
profits were turned. All roads leading to power and wealth were
guided by the same equation.

The Hindu Raj was more or less already in place. All that
remained was to stretch one's patience for a few more riots, a bit
more bloodshed, and the completion of a single temple.

THIRTY-ONE

Rahul and O.P. were eating dinner in the hostel dining hall. It was about nine thirty at night. It seemed Balbir was happy about something; he'd been serving roti, puffed up and piping hot, tinda and potatoes, and channa dal. O.P. ate a lot of raw green chilies.

Suddenly they heard a commotion coming from outside.

O.P. and Rahul ran out to find a group of boys circled around Pratap, Kartikeya, Parvez, Masood, and Praveen.

As soon as Pratap saw Rahul he shouted, "C'mon over here, yaar! And bring your 'superstar' with you too."

O.P. had beaten him to it and had already joined them in the middle of the circle.

The news was that the students from the hostel had, once again, beaten up Lacchu Guru, right in the middle of town, no less, in front of the Ganesh Talkies. This was the revenge for what they'd done to Niketan and Masood.

The whole idea had been Kartikeya's and Pratap's, and they'd been backed up by ten members of the SMTF. The plan was to send Masood and Niketan into the cinema while Kartikeya, Pratap, Parvez, Praveen, Niranjan, Ataluri, and the rest would wait in front outside in a parked Tempo minibus. As soon as Masood and Niketan took out their wallets at the ticket window, two individuals appeared on either side and a scuffle broke out. When Masood began showing some moves, the two of them started to get tougher.

"Guru! The sisterfucker ain't playin' nice," one of them screamed.

"So the Muslim fucker eats halal cow and now he thinks he's Gabbar Khan?" the other screamed.

Lacchu Guru was sitting on the bench next to the paan stall with another sidekick. They sprang up to help.

The boys sitting in the Tempo saw their chance, and the attack was on—with Lacchu Guru once again the target.

In less than ten minutes Lacchu was writhing on the ground, his comrade was begging for mercy, and the other two had fled.

Two policemen were sitting in a nearby tea stall. Each tilted his bald head upward to the sky. That's where Aishwarya Rai was smiling with her fair-colored, lusty eyes, hands raised above her head, underarms exposed. When she arrived in Delhi, the tricolor Indian flag flapped from a mast fastened to the car carrying Miss World. The prime minister and president had photos taken with her. The four lions of the Ashoka Pillar lapped at the soles of her feet. From inside the poster pasted beside the Ganesh Talkies, Miss World's breasts, midriff, and underarms beckoned the town's citizenry: "Give me your money, I'll show you my bunny."

"The two goondas who ran off must have gone straight to Lacchu Guru's big brother's place. Right to Lakhan Lal Pandey's, head of the town council. So we came back here as fast as we could."

"We really hit them where it hurts. Next time they'll think twice before laying a hand on someone from the hostel," Pratap said excitedly.

"VC Agnihotri and the other officials will also get the message. If they only want to listen to the criminals and the goondas, we'll show them we're just as tough," Kartikeya said.

There was an air of festivity that night.

The next day *Janvani*, the so-called national but actually local newspaper, ran a page-one headline that read, "Hooliganism by University Students Causes Anguish to Town Residents." According to the article, many "criminal type" students were inhabiting the university hostels. Dangerous firearms were being amassed in several rooms. According to reliable sources, some students were secret Pakistani ISI agents and members of Naxalite factions. The students were also connected to the smuggling and sale of narcotics.

The article also gave an account of the incident of the night before. Some students with concealed weapons launched an attack on family members of the current head of the town council, Mr. Lakhan Lal Pandey, in the Ganesh Talkies cinema. The head of the Municipal Business Association, Mr. Lakshpati Lal Pandey has been admitted to the local hospital. His condition is said to be stable and not life threatening.

Lastly, an appeal was made to VC Agnihotri and the superintendent of police by certain "eminent" citizens that concrete actions be taken with all deliberate haste and grant the peace-loving citizens of the town greater law and order. The article was signed by reporter Rajeev Shukla.

On page three of the newspaper, which bears the masthead of "Education, Culture, and Entertainment," was an article in praise of Vice-Chancellor Agnihotri by Dr. Chandramani Upadhyay. Also included was a poem by the VC's brother, Prashant Agnihotri, a short travel memoir by the VC's personal secretary M. L. Soni, and an opinion column entitled "Language and Globalization" by the VC's accountant.

It's safe to say that the tattered editor of that newspaper will get sloshed on Chivas Regal tonight in the Asiana's "family cabin no. two," eating so much there's not even room to belch.

Shit! What kind of world are we living in? Rahul thought.

Shaligaram, Shailendra George, and Rahul were all in the same boat in the Hindi department. They went to the Hindi literature section at the library and did a survey, by caste, of the names of the authors of the books. They then moved to periodicals and did the same with the writers and editors of the newspapers and journals. They underlined the names and noted the castes of poets and writers who'd received literary prizes, and the individuals who had awarded them. They compiled a list of who held office and who was ordinary staff for all institutions, academies, and the like associated with the world of Hindi literature. They closely examined the names of reporters, editors, bureau chiefs, and producers of TV and print media.

There couldn't possibly be another place on this planet where one gang of caste members has seized control of an entire language.

"It is a *total solar eclipse* of literature, culture, and language here in this country!"

No one actually uttered this sentence, but any number of varieties, framed with different words, but all with the same meaning, echoed in the heads of Shailendra George, Shaligaram, and Rahul.

Rahul's financial situation was going downhill. Every couple of days someone would show up and inform Rahul that they'd been forbidden to continue private tutoring with him. He hadn't been able to pay his dining hall bill for two months. Even his toothpaste was running low, and he borrowed detergent from O.P. to wash his clothes.

Yesterday had been Thursday, and in spite of everything turned upside down, the organic timepiece in Rahul's heart had been beating through every second in wait: tick-tick, tick-tick.

And at such a moment this love had chosen to come into his life! In his whole life, it was the first such wondrous, magical sensation! Time and again the yellow butterfly disappeared into the darkness and fog that crept through those days.

Two days earlier, Hemant Barua had treated everyone in the dining hall. He'd accepted an offer from IBM, dropping out of the PhD program in mathematics. "What can I do? And besides, what kind of scholar was I really going to make?" He was very pleased. He was offered a yearly salary of 900,000 rupees, after first being sent on a three-month training course.

"I'll write emails from California, and you guys had better write back," Hemant said with a touch of sadness in his otherwise shining eyes. "Let's see if Americans have any free time to play chess."

Then he took Rahul aside and said, "I'm leaving in ten days, so take what I have to say very seriously. Get yourself out of this gutter. I've warned you from the beginning, and I've given you all the data. You will neither get a job in this Hindi business, nor will you become an author. *You are a neoromantic idealistic simpleton."*

Hemant thought a bit more and continued. "You're not going to like this, and I couldn't decide whether or not it was best to spell it out for you. *But I'm your friend and really love you.* So here it is. The truth is that you're never going to get this girl you're chasing after and, by the way, also gambling your life with. You'll end up on the losing end. Mark my words: when it comes time for her to make a choice, she won't choose you, she'll choose someone from her own caste. Get yourself out of here, Rahul. You've become their walking target," Hemant said. He began to get choked up, and his eyes filled with tears.

THIRTY-TWO

O.P. had already dozed off, but that night, in Tagore Hostel Room 252, where Madhuri Dixit once resided in the window, turning her neck to gaze at Rahul with her mad, intoxicated, dumb doe-like eyes and her hit-by-a-slingshot wounded, fleshy back—sleep wouldn't come to Rahul.

A patch of yellow had been inhabiting the same window for several months, which bobbed its way on the winding road up from the valley, first as a tiny, fluttering butterfly and later transforming itself into a yellow parasol. Now on the other side of that window lay a darkness filled with fear, tension, despair, defeat—and silence.

A couple of dim stars tried to twinkle somewhere far off in the distance. The drowsy chirp of a restless bird tossed and turned over the uneasy sound of a cricket symphony.

Rahul was passing through a period of torment filled with deep hostility. Why can't I change how I see things? Why is my heart causing me so much grief, biting me like a cobra again and again? Why do I even bother with this impossible, idiotic, and bloody attempt to discover what might still be alive in something fossilized thousands of years ago in a rough, ugly time? Why am I the one sabotaging my own destiny?

Rahul sat up in bed, reached for the table lamp, and angled it

so he could read a few pages of "How Rama Worshipped Shakti"
in the dim fifteen-watt light.

A curse on this life that's brought me nothing but frustration!
A curse on this discipline for which I've sacrificed!
Janaki! Beloved, alas, I could not rescue you."
But Rama's spirit, tireless, was of another sort,
that knew not meekness, knew not how to beg . . .

Rahul's eyes were moist as he turned the pages.

And Ravana, Ravana, vile wretch, committing atrocities . . .

The tears in his eyes blurred his vision. Why had the person
who'd written these lines been so seething? The words cast their
spell over Rahul. The reader of these poems was none other than
Rahul's very essence, opening the meaning of each word with a
small explosion.

I'm not sure whether this thing inside of me is love or hate for
you, Miss Joshi! Whatever the case, I shall be waiting for you
tomorrow morning.

Please, do come.

THIRTY-THREE

Rahul had filled O.P. in on everything. He was so excited it was as if his own long-awaited dusky she-elf were coming to visit. "I'll padlock the door from the outside and come back at four thirty. Don't worry about anything, yaar!" said the six-foot-three ostrich, wiggling his camel-like neck back and forth.

And it was the camel who had bought, with his own money, a little plastic "packet." For the last six days, Rahul had stood in front of the chemist's, hand in pocket. But in the end, out of embarrassment, he couldn't go through with it, and had returned empty handed.

Rahul playfully hopped onto the back of the camel and swung from his neck, exclaiming, "My dear bony fellow, I can't quite figure out who I love more, you or her!"

"Mogambo khush hua! Mogambo happy man! Heh heh heh heh," gushed the camel.

Anjali was going to set off from the department as soon as Padmashree Tiwari's Vidyapati class ended. Rahul didn't have to go to the department today. Anjali, however, had to first take the road surrounding the sports field, go between the two rocky overhangs behind the equipment storeroom, get through the bushes, and then very carefully climb up the hill to make sure no one saw her.

The back door of Tagore Hostel, always locked, had been left open by O.P. Anjali was to use the back stairs to get to the second floor, then keep by the side wall of the hallway and make her way to Room 252. At that hour all of the students were in class, and the doors to their rooms were padlocked. But if, by chance, someone appeared, Anjali could boldly put on an act, carefree, fully self-confident, since O.P. would simply tell the boy that Anjali was his sister.

Padmashree Rajendra Tiwari's class ended at eleven thirty, so Anjali could be expected by noon.

Rahul was in a state of nervous excitement. As if a top were spinning inside of him. Or a toy jumping dog were leaping around, ceaselessly, since its coil was perpetually wound. Rahul's heart was racing with the same speed as when he watched from his window for the yellow parasol bobbing its way up from the valley. And now, too, the sound of his heartbeat reached right to his ears. Tick-tick, tick-tick.

But was it love or malice thumping in his heart for Anjali? He himself didn't know.

And exactly at five minutes past twelve, she arrived. Her face looked dipped in copper from the sun and fatigue and she was out of breath and exhausted.

O.P. had filled up the thermos with chai and placed a packet of sugar biscuits next to it. In one fluid motion he scooped up the padlock from the table, flashed Rahul a quick smile, left the room, and closed the door behind him. Then came the sounds of O.P. fastening the bolt from the outside, and his footsteps trailing down the hallway.

As he left, the dear camel bellowed a tune in a frightfully off-key voice.

My crazy heart—but where's my sweetie!
It's crazy—from explaining!

Rahul looked at Anjali, who was enthusiastically looking around Rahul's room. "So, Miss Joshi, here you are . . . finally," Rahul said.

"You have no idea! It wasn't easy. The path was awful, and I kept slipping," Anjali said, beaming with a smile of success. She flipped her sandals off. "Look, it broke," she said, pointing at her sandal. Her feet were covered in dirt. Then she twisted her elbow around to show Rahul.

He winced. Her elbow was completely scratched up and bleeding.

"Get me the Dettol," Anjali said, as if she were in her own house and knew a bottle of Dettol was kept on the middle shelf on the left side of the cabinet.

But: there wasn't Dettol. Rahul grabbed a can of aftershave spray, took hold of her arm and pushed the nozzle . . . *pffffffffffff.*

Anjali gritted her teeth. The aftershave spray sharply stung the fresh wound.

Rahul looked at her again. Her hair was a mess, and she was clearly tired. There was a cut on her big toe, her elbow was scraped up, yet there was such a look of innocence on her face, a kind of singular tranquility seen on someone who's finally found their way back home after an arduous, tortuous, strange, meandering journey.

"Where's your parasol?" Rahul asked with some surprise.

"I hid it under that bush."

"What if someone finds it?" This clearly troubled Rahul a bit.

"No one will find it." Anjali was certain.

"What makes you so sure?"

"What do you mean what? I said so, didn't I? No one will find it," Anjali replied.

Tiny bells of laughter rang inside Rahul for no reason at all. He took Anjali's hand into his own, and that's all it took. The electromagnetic cloud burst inside of him; the two began to soar within its field. Rahul kissed each of Anjali's eyes, then her forehead. The storm gathered itself into a whirlwind. Anjali and Rahul's lips explored each other's faces, searching for something.

"This is O.P.'s bed," Rahul said, breathing heavily.

"What!?" Anjali said, quickly getting up. Rahul pulled her down onto his bed.

"So is this the window where you used to . . . ?" Anjali asked.

"Yes—this is the window where your yellow parasol meandered," Rahul said, covering it.

And suddenly he realized that the two of them, even when out in the open, under the sky, on campus, had never felt so free as they did now. Was it possible that the outside world was more constricting than this little tiny room whose door was closed and locked from the outside?

Anjali looked at Rahul so intensely her eyes penetrated his face. She clasped her hands around the base of his neck, drew herself up, and began kissing him.

Just then Hemant's words flashed through Rahul's mind. Is it true that I'm just a sentimental clown who will be left with nothing? *I'm always a loser.* When it comes time to make a choice between one of her own caste and me, she'll choose one of her own. She'll take power, not me! Why? Because she is the daughter of L. K. Joshi, a cabinet minister of this corrupt government, and a Brahmin. It's the same caste whose wicked reign has been like a curse to me and millions of others like me. They're the same "critters" who have for centuries created this unjust, corrupt, gluttonous, vile hell on earth. They are the children of Ravana who kidnapped Sita, destroying Ram's life in exile from his kingdom.

The terrifying faces of Acharya S. N. Mishra and Balram Pandey leered at him from above, both of whom wore moustaches like tiny black moths seated below their noses in the style of the Führer. It was the same fear that prevented him from sleeping that night. These conspiratorial, indestructible hypocrites ripped people like Rahul out of the ground and with a snap of their fingers threw them away like a simple blade of grass.

The fish in Rahul's arms got agitated. The little red river running through the veins of his body where, up until a few seconds ago, had been playing a sweet-sounding melody for two teeny-tiny shining swimming fish, now portended a maelstrom. His hand advanced to her shirt, where he started jerking open the buttons.

"Wait, wait, what are you doing, Rahul?" Anjali wanted to grab his wrist. Her appeal was in vain, since by now her shirt was totally unbuttoned. Rahul's hands were insistent.

"Rahul!" Anjali said, her voice cracking. "What are you doing? Please! Why are you in a hurry?"

"Because I'm not Rahul, I'm a leopard, a panther," he said as he unzipped her jeans.

The leopard attacked his prey with full ferocity. Anjali stopped resisting. She gazed with the startled eyes of a doe at the animal atop her.

"Girls like to be roughed up, don't they? They're aching for Shahrukh Khan, aren't they? The guy who he played in *Darr*." Or, Salman Khan, who eats deer—Black Buck.

A fierce storm and the excitement of a wild, vicious animal surged together inside Rahul. With all the strength he could muster, he took revenge for centuries of injustice against downtrodden castes. Thup, thup, thup. His every thrust was a sting of revenge; his every movement part of the business of payback.

Anjali's eyes were half closed, her mouth hung open, and her face glowed like hot embers.

It surprised him that as his vengeance on behalf of the oppressed castes grew deeper and sharper, Anjali's eyes showed a look of near bliss, while her lips drew into the outline of a faint smile. "Oh, oh!"

A scene from that movie flashed in Rahul's mind—no, it was a novel, Coetzee's novel, *In the Heart of the Country*, the part when the black servant, after killing his white master, takes revenge for centuries of slavery and oppression of the black race by raping his daughter. But his revenge turns out to be something pleasurable for the girl.

Is it possible that Anjali . . . ? At the very heart of her biological makeup she's inherited genes that make her prone to be a pleasure-seeking sensualist—hedonism is present in her DNA. Isn't it possible she traveled all this way, braved rocky roads, climbed over hills, whacked her way through thorny thickets, just to get to this room, just to get her kicks and have some fun?

Rahul was suddenly swept with a strange feeling of inferiority. What if he was just a pleasure-giving plaything to her? Just some sex toy? A dildo?

Rahul was nearly at a loss. The leopard gathered every last bit of strength in his body and pushed for one more attack.

"You are really insane," Anjali said afterward. "You said that you'd 'arranged' everything. Now look—what if something happens?"

Rahul experienced an entirely new sensation from the way she was looking at him. Her eyes shone with guilelessness, suggesting their deep physical intimacy, and it was a look she'd never given him before.

Rahul's gaze fell on the bedsheets; there was Anjali's blood. A lot of it. He looked at Anjali, froze, and stopped thinking altogether. It was like a blow to the senses.

She was looking at him with an unwavering gaze of deep maternal affection and warmth, her eyes brimming with the twinkle of a faraway star.

Her elbow was cut up, her feet were bruised, her sandal had broken, the bedsheets were soaked in blood, and on top of it all the scratches and fingernail marks on her back and arms, all of which she'd endured without so much as a peep, and now she was looking at him with such a deep, wordless compassion, sensuality, and tenderness. They were the eyes of some small child, incredibly innocent, free from the foul and filth and shame of the times. They were like newly sprouted, fully formed blossoms.

Rahul placed his head into Anjali's lap and began to cry like a baby. Anjali kissed his forehead continually. She cradled his head in her arms and tried to calm him. She still wasn't wearing any clothes; her thighs, stomach, and breasts were moistened by Rahul's tears. His teardrops mixed with the blood and come on the bedsheet.

"Why are you crying? Shhhhh . . . shhhhhhh. Someone might hear." Anjali couldn't understand why Rahul was crying. She kept repeating, "You are a real clown! Johnny Joker. My crazy boy."

Finally she guessed why Rahul was crying and began to kiss his forehead. "Listen! I really do love you, you know. No one can separate us, I promise. Now please calm down."

"Please, calm down!" Anjali said more loudly, teasing him, without caring that her voice was a girl's voice that could carry outside, a voice that had never been heard coming from a room in this hostel.

Rahul became frightened. He kissed Anjali and began to laugh. A laugh on a helpless face covered in tears, anguish, and regret.

That Thursday, until four o'clock in the afternoon, Rahul and Anjali made love two more times with impatience and longing to be united with one another, as if they were two little fish swimming toward one another in a choppy sea. A pure, primal, ancient, eternal, natural impatience.

THIRTY-FOUR

The story after this becomes very brief for the reason that it's not something that took place once upon a time, long, long ago. The story is, in fact, just a fraction of a larger narrative that is still taking place, even today. It's a work in progress, a tale that's under construction, a report of what just happened one second ago in a life very much still being lived.

Anjali came to Rahul's room three more times over the next month in the same manner: under the radar, clawing her way through the thicket, stumbling over rocky ridges, with a broken sandal, banged-up body, torn clothing, and a sunburned, exhausted-looking face huffing and puffing away. This was the condition of Anjali Joshi, daughter of the cabinet minister, billionaire builder, and Brahmin by caste L. K. Joshi.

Were these two trapped inside a clichéd Bollywood screenplay, waiting for the shoe to drop, like in the formulaic tragedies popular in the '6os of poor boy–rich girl romance?

During that month, the police came at night and conducted a cordon-and-search operation. Half a dozen rooms were searched. Kartikeya Kajle, Masood, Praveen, Madhusudan, D. Gopal Rajulu, and Akhilesh Ranjan were taken by the police. Luckily, Rahul's room had not been raided; maybe he'd been spared since Pratap Parihar's uncle was a police officer.

Two days later, Praveen, Gopal Rajulu, and Madhusudan returned to the hostel. The police had beaten them and let them go, while Kartikeya, Masood, and Akhilesh Ranjan remained under arrest.

The oversized headline on page one of *Janvani* screamed, "Stockpile of Weapons and Contraband Recovered from Student Hostel: Three Arrested." Praveen reported that first the police, then Lacchu Guru, beat up Kartikeya until he was in sad shape. They broke Masood's kneecaps. The policed brandished the fake evidence they'd planted; meanwhile, they'd failed to find the pistol that was actually hidden in Pratap's room.

Madhusudan said that Kartikeya had cried his eyes dry. He'd been preparing to take the civil service exam; now his entire future was ruined. The head of the municipality, Lakkhu Bhaiya, and the state cabinet minister Joshi were behind the whole thing. It was only after the VC had given his blessing that the police entered the university hostel. They were kept in custody, and, not only were they charged with selling narcotics and possession of illegal weapons, but the crimes they were charged with were additionally subject to counterterrorism laws.

The same day, an English-language newspaper published a front-page photo of a young Sikh who had been a victim of police harassment standing in front of the Supreme Court in Delhi. He had poured gasoline over his body and had set fire to himself. In the photograph, both of his arms were raised in the air as the flames engulfed him. There was a small crowd of spectators watching nearby. In the background was the highest court of this country.

A seminar had been organized in the Hindi department during that time. The topic of the first session was "Instances of Mannerism in Contemporary Poetry" and the topic of the second, "The Question of the Autonomy of Literature." Dr. Jarihar Dwivedi, Dr. Sohan Lal Chaturvedi, Dr. Marudhar Pandey, Professor Ajayab Aggrawal, and K. L. Vajpayee came from Delhi to attend. In addition, some dozen poets arrived in the state capital cities like Lucknow, Patna, and Bhopal. Save one or two, all of the poets' names ended with caste surnames like Shukla, Tiwari, Pandey, Joshi, "Aal-Waal," and Sharma.

They were given fare for air-conditioned passage, travel allowance and expense allowance, a bouquet of flowers, and, on top of that, a 7,000-rupee honorarium. The Hindi department, in cooperation with the state ministry for culture, made all the arrangements and ran up a total bill of some 500,000 rupees.

The letter of invitation to the seminar, the lovely program of events, and the participants' souvenir were all printed by the *Janvani* printing press.

THIRTY-FIVE

When Anjali visited Room 252 of Tagore hostel for the fourth time, after O.P. had padlocked the room until four o'clock and left singing in his special camel-like style, as Rahul took Anjali's hand into his, and their fingers became entangled, until both of their bodies were enveloped by an electromagnetic storm, or swept up in a twister, or tossed by big waves in an unsettled sea in which they'd shed their clothing, and as they were beginning to swim like two tiny fish crashing into one another in an attempt to pierce one another through and through, just then . . .

. . . there was a knocking noise. Anjali and Rajul froze and looked up.

In the ventilation space above the door were two faces. One of the faces belonged to hostel warden Chandramani Upadhyay's servant, and the other to Gopal Dwivedi. It was the same Gopal Dwivedi who had spoken with Acharya S. N. Mishra and secured Rahul's admission to the Hindi department. "Esteemed brother," he had called him. Rahul shuddered. These were the very eyes underneath which was the nose that sheltered the infamous black moth of a moustache made notorious during the 1930s and '40s. It was frightening, like an evil omen.

The two covered themselves with the bedsheet.

The faces vanished from the ventilation space.

The worst of it was nothing could be done: the door was padlocked from the outside. O.P. had locked it, and wouldn't be back until four o'clock.

Sometime around two-thirty the sound of footsteps was heard somewhere outside; it was the sound of feet marching closer, until they stopped in front of the door. The key turned in the lock; it snapped open; the sound of the latch handle squeaking. The door opened.

The six-foot-three ostrich stood outside; his face was drained of color. His heron-like neck was totally rigid with fear. His lips were quivering. Five others were with him: warden Dr. Chandramani Upadhyay, Anjali's brother D. K. Joshi, and three unknown individuals—massive, flat-faced characters.

"Come." Anjali's brother flatly issued this directive in a voice like cold iron.

Anjali grabbed her bag from the table and quietly exited. Rahul stood in the middle of the room.

The others escorted Anjali away. Her brother D. K. Joshi and O.P. remained standing in the doorway. Looking at Rahul with eyes at once cold and penetrating to his very core, the former said: "I don't want to 'create' a 'scene.' This is a question of honor. But you'd better think twice before making a move. Keep your mouth shut. If you try to do anything nasty, you'll end up as a corpse in the city hospital waiting for a postmortem in the same place as that little monkey motherfucker Sapam."

Having said this, he turned and left. After a few steps he spun around to add, "Did my words sink into that head of yours? Think before you act." And he continued on his way.

O.P. looked at Rahul with deeply frightened eyes.

THIRTY-SIX

And now, the part of this unfinished tale that can be reported in any fashion.

This is a train. A Rajdhani Express. Train no. 2002. Anjali Joshi and Rahul are occupying berths 41 and 42 in compartment N-8. It is nighttime, and the clock reads eleven twenty-three. The Rajdhani Express is racing along at a fast clip.

There's no sleepiness in Anjali and Rahul's eyes. They're looking at each other, wide awake. It seems that the very reason they're awake is because they need to keep looking at one another.

Today is Anjali's birthday. She's a Capricorn.

Abha, Anima, Sharmistha, Neera Didi, Parvez, Pratap, Shailendra George, Shaligaram, Seema Philip, Chandra . . . they were all in on the conspiracy that, under the pretense of a night at the movies for her birthday, plotted to spring Anjali from a monthlong house arrest. During the intermission at eight thirty, Anjali snuck out under a shawl to cover her face and got herself to the train station. Neither she nor Rahul, who had arrived first, was alone. The whole flock of conspiratorial friends was with them at the station, including the six-foot ostrich.

There wasn't a hint of fear on any of their faces; rather, they showed strength, smarts, resolve, and joy, and their eyes twinkled with compassion. As the train pulled out of the station they all jumped up and down and waved their hands to bid them farewell.

Rahul and Anjali remained standing in the doorway, watching, until the train had gone some distance. Until his tears of gratitude and ecstasy erected a wall of water in front of his eyes, Rahul kept his eyes fixed on the smiling, wagging head that was fixed atop the longest, heron-like neck.

This journey was uncertain, but full of hope and longing. Rahul and Anjali stared at each other, never blinking, with the fixed posture of two celestial bodies.

It was five minutes to two in the morning when they heard the screeching sound of the train braking. After sliding down the tracks a bit, the carriages came to a halt. They'd stopped in the middle of nowhere; it was totally dark outside. Maybe someone had pulled the emergency chain, or the train engineer had received a red stop signal.

Suddenly there was a loud racket. Someone was forcing their way in the carriage by first banging on and then succeeding to break through the door. A dozen or so people barged into the compartment N-8, all bearing weapons. Their faces were flat. Two of them came forward and grabbed hold of Anjali. Another quickly covered her in a black blanket, scooped her up like a bundle and, in the blink of an eye, whisked her away.

Several people pounced on Rahul. Someone had switched off the main circuit breaker, and the entire compartment was plunged into darkness. Three or four people had seized Rahul, who was struggling to break free. He realized someone had leaked the information. Was all lost?

Through the darkness, Rahul could see a man bring in a big tin bucket and set it on the ground. Some wood was put into it and something like ghee was dumped in with the wood. A match was lit, it was set on fire, and the flames began shooting up.

A dark face with a ceremonial tilak mark of sandalwood paste on his forehead, black moth moustache, caveman-like apparition flickered in the flames.

Om bhuh swaha idamagnaye na mam
Om bhuh swaha idam vayave na mam
Om bhuh swaha idam brahmane na mam

The scary gorilla was chanting a mantra and stoking the fire with something. The flames leaped higher and higher.

The rest of the people were seated in a circle around the raging inferno. They had placed their guns, switchblades, swords, and billy clubs on the ground next to them and, god knows how, but they all now had books in their hands.

Om bhuh swaha idam na mam

Rahul saw one of them who was holding a copy of the Rigveda rip out a page and toss it in the fire . . . *swaha!*

Another was stoking the fire with pages from Marx's *Das Capital.*

Om bhuh swaha idam na mam

Another had a copy of the works of Gandhi.

Om bhuh swaha

Then they all ripped out pages and stoked the fire with Lohia, Narendra Dev, Buddhist scriptures, the Bible, the Quran.

Om bhuh
Om bhuh swaha
Swaha! Swaha!

The flames began licking the roof of the compartment. People who'd been sleeping on the upper berths jumped down and began to flee. At the other end were commandos armed with AK-47s.

Just then Rahul saw the potbellied goonda, broker, and rich-looking man stand up, just as fat, frightening, and loose as ever. He had his cell phone out and was dialing a number. "Hello! Hello! I'm Nikhlani here! Speaking on behalf of the IMF! Get me to the prime minister, okay?! Ask him to call me back on my mobile!"

He switched off his cell phone, picked up a long machete from the ground, and advanced toward Rahul.

Om! Bhuh swaha idam na mam! swaha!

Rahul was still being restrained at berth 42 by four men. The fat man slowly raised the blade of the machete . . . Rahul froze in terror.

This was Parashuram, barbarous and cruel. His machete was covered in blood. It was the same one he used to separate his own mother's head from the trunk of her body. But she had ten heads. Wait, that was Ravana . . .

In a split second death from machete would fall on Rahul's neck.

That split second was upon him.

Tick, tick, tick. The clock made of flesh in his heart was still ticking, and two tiny golden fish were still swimming in the red river of his veins. Two eyes, wet with tears, unblinking like stars . . .

The machete fell on his neck. Rahul resisted with all his strength and screamed, "Hé Raaaaaaaam!"

His eyes sprang open. Anjali was planting kisses on his head and giggling. "So *this* is how you sleep? If I hadn't grabbed hold of you, you would have fallen right off the berth onto the ground!" Anjali said. "You are really a crazy one, aren't you!"

The light of the dawn was shimmering in through the window. The pleasant, murmuring warmth of the winter sun.

UDAY PRAKASH is one of contemporary Hindi's most important voices. Considered one of India's most original and audacious writers, he is among the most popular authors in India nowadays. Prakash's texts describe the ongoing transformations of the contemporary Indian society.

Prakash is not an uncontroversial figure in the world of Hindi literature. He has been attacked from all parts of the political spectrum for his very individual approaches to the contradictory manifestations of modernity in contemporary Indian society as well as the challenges posed by the Hindi literary establishment to younger writers who wish to do new things with language and form.

Prakash is the author of poems, short stories, non-fiction, films, and documentaries. In 2010 he received the prestigious Sahitya Akademi literary award, one of India's highest literary honors. He is professor-in-charge, Department of Mass Communication, Media, and Journalism, Indira Gandhi Tribal University, Amarkantak. He lives in Ghaziabad, India.

JASON GRUNEBAUM grew up in Buffalo, New York. He earned an MFA in fiction from Columbia University, and is currently Senior Lecturer in Hindi at the University of Chicago, where he also teaches creative writing. His stories and translations have appeared in many literary journals.

Grunebaum has been awarded an NEA Literature Fellowship and a PEN Translation Fund grant. His "Maria Ximenes da Costa de Carvalho Perreira" was selected by Salman Rushdie for a Best American Short Stories honorable mention. Grunebaum has also translated Prakash's "The Walls of Delhi," which was shortlisted for the 2013 DSC Prize in South Asian Literature.